SEASON OF SECRETS

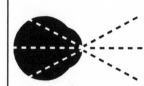

This Large Print Book carries the
Seal of Approval of N.A.V.H.

SEASON OF SECRETS

MARTA PERRY

THORNDIKE PRESS

An imprint of Thomson Gale, a part of The Thomson Corporation

NEW HANOVER COUNTY
PUBLIC LIBRARY
201 CHESTNUT STREET
WILMINGTON, NC 28401

THOMSON

GALE

Detroit • New York • San Francisco • New Haven, Conn. • Waterville, Maine • London

LIBRARY OF CONGRESS CATALOGING-IN-PUBLICATION DATA

Perry, Marta.
    Season of secrets / by Marta Perry.
       p. cm. — (Thorndike Press large print Christian mystery)
    ISBN-13: 978-1-4104-0274-5 (alk. paper)
    ISBN-10: 1-4104-0274-6 (alk. paper)
    1. Large type books. I. Title.
    PS3616.E7933S43 2007
    813'.6—dc22   2007030258

Published in 2007 by arrangement with Harlequin Books S.A.

Printed in the United States of America on permanent paper
10 9 8 7 6 5 4 3 2 1

For now we see in a mirror, darkly, but then face to face; now I know in part, but then I shall know full, even as I am known.

— *1 Corinthians* 13:12

This story is dedicated to my
granddaughter,
Greta Nicole Wulff, with much love
from Grammy.
And, as always, to Brian.

ONE

"Why is he coming back now?"

Aunt Kate put her morning cup of Earl Grey back in the saucer as she asked the question for what had to be the twentieth time since they'd heard the news, her faded blue eyes puckered with distress. December sunlight streamed through the lace curtains on the bay window in the breakfast room, casting into sharp relief the veins that stood out on her hand, pressed to the polished tabletop.

"I don't know, Aunt Kate."

Love swept through Dinah Westlake, obliterating her own fears about Marc Devlin's return to Charleston. She covered the trembling hand with her own, trying to infuse her great-aunt with her own warmth. Anger sparked. Marc shouldn't come back, upsetting their lives once again.

"Maybe he just wants to sell the house since the Farriers moved out." Aunt Kate sounded hopeful, and she glanced toward the front window and the house that stood across the street in the quiet Charleston historic block.

Annabel's house. The house where Annabel died.

Dinah forced herself to focus on the question. "I suppose so. Do you know if he's bringing Court?"

Her cousin Annabel's son had been three when she'd seen him last, and now he was thirteen. She remembered a soft, cuddly child who'd snuggled up next to her, begging for just one more bedtime story. It was unlikely that Courtney would want or need anything from her now.

"I don't know." Aunt Kate's lips firmed into a thin line. "I hope not."

Dinah blinked. "Don't you want to see Courtney?" This visit was the first indication that Marc would let his son have a relationship with his mother's kin that consisted of more than letters, gifts and brief thank-you notes.

Tears threatened to spill over onto her great-aunt's soft cheeks. "Of course I do. But that poor child shouldn't be exposed to the house where his mother died, even if it means I never see him again."

"Aunt Kate —" Dinah's words died. She

couldn't say anything that would make a difference, because she understood only too well what her aunt felt. She, too, had not been back in that house since Annabel's funeral.

Except in the occasional nightmare. Then, she stood again on the graceful curving staircase of Annabel and Marc's house, looking down toward the dim hallway, hearing angry voices from the front parlor. Knowing something terrible was about to happen. Unable to prevent it.

"Everyone will start talking about Annabel's death again." Aunt Kate touched a lacy handkerchief to her eyes, unable as always to say the uglier word. Murder. "Just when it's forgotten, people will start to talk again."

Something recoiled in Dinah. It seemed so disloyal never to talk about Annabel. Still, if that was how Aunt Kate dealt with the pain, maybe it was better than having nightmares.

She slid her chair back, patting her aunt's hand. "Don't worry about it too much. I'm sure people are so busy getting ready for the Christmas holidays that Marc will have been and gone before anyone takes notice."

Her aunt clasped her hand firmly. "You're not going to the office today, are you? Dinah, you have to stay home. What if he

11

comes?"

It was no use pointing out to her that Dinah was going to police headquarters, not an office. Aunt Kate couldn't possibly refer to her as a forensic artist. In Aunt Kate's mind, a Charleston lady devoted herself to the church, charity and society, not necessarily in that order.

"I thought I'd check in this morning." As a freelance police artist she only worked when called on, but she'd found it helped her acceptance with the detectives to remind them of her presence now and then.

"Please, Dinah. Stay home today."

Her hesitation lasted only an instant. Aunt Kate had taken care of her. Now it was her turn. She bent to press her cheek against Aunt Kate's.

"Of course I will, if that's what you want. But given the way he's cut ties with us, I don't expect Marcus Devlin to show up on our doorstep anytime soon."

Was she being a complete coward? Maybe so. But she'd fought her way back from the terror of the night Annabel died, and she had no desire to revisit that dreadful time.

Please, God. Please let me forget.

That was a petition that was hardly likely to be granted, now that Marc Devlin was coming home.

■ ■ ■ ■

After helping her aunt to the sunroom that looked over her garden, where she would doze in the winter sunshine, Dinah cleared the breakfast dishes. It was one of the few things Alice Jones, her aunt's devoted housekeeper, allowed her to do to help.

Alice was nearly as old as her great-aunt, and the two of them couldn't hope to stay on in the elegant, inconvenient antebellum house on Tradd Street if she weren't here. She wasn't even sure when she'd gone from being the cosseted little girl of the house to being the caretaker, but she didn't see the situation changing anytime soon, and she wouldn't want it to.

A sound disturbed the morning quiet. Someone wielded the brass dolphin knocker on the front door with brisk energy. It could be anyone. Her stomach tightened; the back of her neck prickled. Instinct said it was Marc.

Heart thudding, she crossed the Oriental carpet that had covered the hall floor for a hundred years or so. She turned the brass doorknob and opened the door.

Instinct was right. Her cousin's husband stood on the covered veranda, hand arrested halfway to the knocker. A shaft of winter sunlight, filtered through the branches of the magnolia tree, struck hair that was still glossy black.

For a moment, Dinah could only stare. It was Marc, of course, but in another sense it wasn't. This wasn't the intent, idealistic young prosecutor her teenage dreams had idolized.

"Dinah." He spoke first, his deep voice breaking the spell that held her silent. "It's been a long time."

"Not by our choice," she said, before thinking about the implication.

The lines around his firm mouth deepened. "I know." He quirked one eyebrow, and the familiar movement broke through her sense of strangeness. "Are you going to let me come in?"

She felt her cheeks warm. What was she doing, keeping him standing on the veranda like a door-to-door salesperson? No matter how much his return distressed Aunt Kate, she couldn't treat him as anything but the cousin-in-law he'd always been to her.

She stepped back. "Please, come in." She grasped for the comfort of ingrained manners. "It's good to see you again, Marc."

He stepped into the wide center hallway, the movement seeming to stir the quiet air, and she had to suppress a gasp as pain gripped her heart. Forgotten? No, she hadn't forgotten at all. His presence brought her ten-year-old grief surging to life.

Was being here doing the same for him? She thought it might — his face had tightened, but that was all. He was better at hiding his feelings than he used to be.

She had to say something, anything, to bridge the silence. She took refuge in the ordinary. "Did you have a pleasant flight?"

He shrugged. "Not bad. I'd forgotten how warm South Carolina can be in December."

"That just shows how much of a Northerner you've become. Everyone here has been complaining that it's too cold."

His face relaxed into a half smile. "Wimp. You should try a Boston winter sometime to see what cold really is."

"No, thanks. I'll pass."

He had changed. He was ten years older, of course. Ten years would change anyone. He looked — successful, she supposed. Dress shirt, dark tie, a tweed jacket that fit smoothly over broad shoulders, a flash of gold at his wrist that was probably an expensive watch. Being a corporate attorney instead of a prosecutor must suit him.

But it wasn't so much the way he was dressed as the air about him — the air of a successful, accomplished man.

"Well?" He lifted that eyebrow again. "What's the verdict, Dinah?"

She wouldn't pretend to misunderstand him. "I was thinking that you talk faster than you used to."

He smiled. "I had to learn because no one would stick around long enough to hear what I had to say."

The smile was a reminder of the Marc she'd known. *Dear Father, this is harder than I'd imagined it could be. Please, get me through it.*

"Come into the parlor." However much she might wish he'd leave, she couldn't stand here in the hall with him.

She turned and walked into the small, perfectly appointed front parlor. He'd find this familiar, she supposed. Aunt Kate hadn't changed anything in seventy years, and she never would. Anything that showed wear was replaced with an exact duplicate. Aunt Kate didn't bother to decorate for Christmas much in recent years, but the white mantel bore its usual evergreen, magnolia leaves and holly, studded with the fat ivory candles that would be lit Christmas Eve.

Dinah sat on the Queen Anne love seat, gesturing to the wing chair opposite. Marc sat, leaning back, seeming very much at ease. But the lines on his face deepened, and his dark eyes hid secrets.

"You've changed." His comment startled her, but it shouldn't. Hadn't she just been thinking the same about him? No one stayed the same for ten years.

"I'm ten years older. That makes a difference." Especially when it was the difference between an immature teen and an adult woman.

He shook his head. "It's not just that. You're not shy anymore."

"I've learned to hide it better, that's all."

Marc *would* remember the shy, gawky teenager she'd once been. She could only hope he'd never noticed the crush she'd had on him.

"It's easy to see that you're blooming. How is Aunt Kate?"

And how, exactly, was she going to explain the fact that Aunt Kate wasn't coming in to greet him?

"She's . . . older, obviously. She'd deny it vehemently, but she's begun to fail a little."

"So you're taking care of her."

"Of course."

That's how it is in families, Marc. We take care of each other. We don't walk away, the way you did.

17

He frowned slightly, and she had the uncomfortable sense that he knew what she was thinking.

"Is she too frail to see me?"

Her careful evasion had led her just where she didn't want to be. "No. She just —"

She faltered to a halt. There wasn't any good way of saying that Aunt Kate didn't welcome his return.

"She just doesn't want to see me." His mouth thinned. "Tell me, does she think I killed Annabel?"

The blunt question shook her, and mentioning Annabel's name seemed to bring her into the room. For an instant Dinah heard the light tinkle of Annabel's laugh, caught a whiff of the sophisticated fragrance that had been Annabel's scent. Grief ripped through her, and she struggled to speak.

"I — I'm sure she doesn't think that." But did she? With her firm avoidance of the subject, Aunt Kate had managed never to say.

His dark gaze seemed to reject the feeble words. "What about you, Dinah? Do you think that?"

Before she could find the words, he shook his head.

"Never mind. I don't suppose it matters."

She found the words then, at the pain in

his voice. "I don't think you could have hurt Annabel."

How could anyone have hurt Annabel, have struck out and destroyed all that life, all that beauty?

His face seemed to relax a fraction. "Thank you. I'm selling the house. I suppose you guessed that."

"We thought that was probably why you'd come back," she said cautiously, not wanting to make it sound as if that was what she wanted.

"It's time. Having the Farriers rent the place all these years let me drift, but when they decided to move, I knew I had to do something about the house."

"You won't be here long, then." She was aware of a sense of relief. He would go away, and the terrible wound of Annabel's death would skin over again.

His brows lifted. "Are you eager to see the last of me, Dinah?"

"No." He was making her feel like that awkward teen again. "I just assumed you'd be in a hurry to get the house on the market and go back to your life, especially with the holidays coming."

"The holidays," he repeated, something a little wary in his voice.

"I suppose you and Court have all sorts

of plans for Christmas." She was talking at random, trying to cover her embarrassment.

"Well, he's past the Santa stage, but he still gets excited."

"Does he?" For a moment she had a vivid image of the three-year-old he'd been — big dark eyes filled with wonder at the smallest things — a butterfly in the garden or a new puzzle she'd bought him, knowing how much he loved working them. "I'd love to see him."

Again the words came out before she considered. Marc had made his wishes clear all these years, limiting their contact to cards and gifts. Just because he'd come back didn't mean anything had changed.

"You'll get your wish," Marc said abruptly. "He's over at the house now, unloading the rental car."

She could only stare at him. "You've brought Court here, to the house where —" She stopped, unable to say the words.

"You think I'm crazy to bring Court back to the house where his mother died." Marc's voice was tinged with bitterness, but he could give voice to the thought she couldn't.

"I'm sorry." She sought refuge in platitudes. "I'm sure you know what's best for your son."

"Do I?" Vulnerability suddenly showed in

his normally guarded eyes, disarming her. "I wish I were sure. I thought I knew. I thought the best thing for Court was a whole new life, with nothing to remind him of what he'd lost."

"So you kept him away from us." Did he have any idea how much that had hurt?

"Away from you, away from this place."

Marc surged to his feet as if he couldn't sit still any longer. He stalked to the window, then turned and came back again. The room seemed too small for him. He stopped in front of her.

"I did what I thought I had to," he said uncompromisingly. "And it worked. Court was a normal, bright, happy kid, too happy and busy to worry about the past."

She caught the tense. "Was?"

"Was." He sat down heavily.

She waited, knowing he'd tell her, whatever it was. She didn't want to hear, she thought in sudden panic. But it was too late for that.

"Maybe this would have happened anyway," he said slowly, sounding as if he tried to be fair. "He's thirteen — it's a tough age. But when school started in September, one of his teachers assigned a writing project on family history. He started asking questions."

"About Annabel."

He nodded. "About her, about her family. About our life here in Charleston. He became obsessed." He stopped, as if he'd heard what he said and wanted it back. "Not obsessed — that's not right. I don't think there's anything unhealthy about it. He's curious. He wants to know."

She swallowed, feeling the lump in her throat at the thought of Annabel's child. "I remember. He was always curious."

"Yes." His face was drawn. "He has to know things. So he told me what he wanted for Christmas."

He paused, and she had a sense of dread at what he was about to say.

"He wanted to come back to Charleston. That's all he asked for. To come back here and have Christmas in the house before I sell it."

"And you said yes."

"What else could I do?" He leaned toward her, his dark eyes focusing on her face, and that sense of dread deepened. "But it's more complicated than I thought."

"What do you mean?"

His hand closed over hers, and she felt his urgency. "I realized something the moment I saw the house again — realized what I've been evading all these years. I have to know the truth about Annabel's death."

He had shocked Dinah, Marc realized. Or maybe *shock* wasn't the right word for her reaction. His years as a prosecutor had taught him to find body language more revealing than speech, and Dinah was withdrawing, protecting herself against him.

Protecting. The word startled him. Dinah didn't have anything to fear from him.

He deliberately relaxed against the back of the chair, giving her space. Wait. See how she responded to that. See if she would help him or run from him.

He glanced around the room with a sense of wonder. It hadn't changed since the days when he'd come here to pick up Annabel, and he'd thought it caught in a previous century then. Clearly Kate preferred things the way they had always been.

But Dinah had changed. He remembered so clearly Annabel's attitude toward her shy young cousin — a mixture of love and a kind of amused exasperation.

She's such a dreamer. Annabel had lifted her hands in an expressive gesture. She's impossibly young for her age, and I don't see how she's ever going to mature, living in that house with Aunt Kate. Let's have her here for the summer. She can help out with Court, and maybe I can help her grow up a little.

His heart caught at the memory. *I feel it more here, Lord. Is that why I had to come back?*

Dinah had certainly grown up. Skin soft as a magnolia blossom, blue-black hair curling to her shoulders, those huge violet eyes. He couldn't describe her without resorting to the classic Southern clichés. Charleston knew how to grow beautiful women.

Dinah seemed to realize how long the silence had grown. She cleared her throat. "I don't know what you hope to accomplish at this late date. The police department considers it an unsolved case. I'm sure someone looks at the file now and then, but —" The muscles in her neck worked, as if she had trouble saying those words.

"They've written it off, you mean. I haven't." He wasn't doing this very well, maybe because he hadn't realized what he really wanted until he'd driven down the street and pointed out the house to his son. "Court hasn't."

Dinah's hands were clasped in her lap, so tightly that the skin strained over her knuckles. "There's nothing left to find after ten years. No one left to talk to about it."

"There's you, Dinah. You were there."

Her face went white with shock, and he knew he'd made a misstep. He shouldn't have rushed things with her, assumed she'd want what he wanted.

She pushed the words away with both hands. "I didn't see anything. I don't know anything. You, of all people, should know that."

A vivid image filled his mind, fresh as if it had happened yesterday — Dinah's small form crumpled on the staircase of the house across the street, black hair spilling around her. He'd found her when he'd come home in the early hours of the morning from a trip to track down a witness in one of his cases.

He'd rushed downstairs to the phone, shouting for Annabel, and seen the light in the parlor still burning. He'd pushed open the half-closed door —

No. He wouldn't let his thoughts go any farther than that. It was too painful, even after all this time.

"I know that you fell, that you had a concussion. That you said you didn't remember anything."

"I didn't. I don't." Anger flared in her face, bringing a flush to her cheeks that wiped away the pallor. "If I knew anything about who killed Annabel, don't you think I'd have spoken up by now? I loved her!"

The words rang in the quiet room. They seemed to hold an accusation.

"I loved her, too, Dinah. Or don't you believe that?"

She sucked in a breath, as if the room had gone airless. "Yes." The word came out slowly, and her eyes were dark with pain. "I believe you loved her. But there's nothing you can do for her now. She's at peace."

"The rest of us aren't." His jaw tightened until it was difficult to force the words out. "Court knows I was a suspect in his mother's death. My son knows that, Dinah."

"Oh, Marc." The pity in her face was almost worse than her anger had been. "I'm sorry. Surely he doesn't believe you did it."

"He says he doesn't." He tried to look at the situation objectively, as if he were a prosecutor assessing a case again. "Most of the time I think that's true."

But what if there was a doubt, even a fraction of a doubt? Could he stand to see his close relationship with his son eroded day by day, month by month, until they were polite strangers?

"I'm sorry," she said again, looking at him as if she knew all the things he didn't say. "I wish I could help you. I really do. But I don't know anything."

He studied her troubled expression. Dinah certainly thought she was telling the truth, but there might be more to it than that. She'd been there, in the house, that whole summer. There far more than he had been, in fact. If there'd been any clue, any small indication of trouble in the events of that summer, Dinah could have seen.

He wouldn't say that to her, not now. He'd shaken her enough already, and if he wanted her cooperation, he'd have to step carefully.

"I understand." He stood, seeing the relief she tried to hide that he was leaving. He held out his hand to her. After a moment she rose, slipping her hand in his. Hers was small and cold in his grip. "But you can still be a friend, can't you? To me and to Court?"

She hesitated for a fraction of an instant before she produced a smile. "Of course. You must know that."

"Good." He made his voice brisk, knowing he had to pin her down while he could. "Come and see us tomorrow. We should be settled enough by then to entertain a guest. I want you to meet Court."

Again that slight hesitation. And then she nodded. "I'll see you tomorrow."

It wasn't much, but it was enough to start

with. If Dinah knew anything, eventually he'd know it, too.

Two

"I just wish you wouldn't go over there."
Aunt Kate followed Dinah to the front hall
the next day as if she'd bar the door.

Dinah stopped, managing a smile for her
great-aunt. "I wish I didn't have to." She
hadn't told Aunt Kate about Marcus's
intention of looking into Annabel's death.
That would only distress her more.

"Well, then —"

"I must, don't you see?" Obviously Aunt
Kate didn't, or they wouldn't be having this
conversation again. "You're the one who
taught me about the importance of family."

Aunt Kate's lips pursed into a shape
reminiscent of a bud on one of her rose-
bushes. "Marcus Devlin is not a member of
our family."

"Annabel was." She struggled to say the
words evenly.

Aunt Kate's eyes misted. "Does he know
you haven't been in that house since Anna-

bel died?"

"No. And you're not to tell him." She clutched Aunt Kate's hand. "Promise me."

"Of course, dear. But if it bothers you that much, it's all the more reason not to become involved with Marcus's visit."

"This isn't about Marcus. I have to go over there for Court's sake."

Aunt Kate gave in at that — she could see it in her eyes. It was a good thing, because Dinah couldn't bear to argue with her.

"I suppose if you must, you must." She touched Dinah's hair lightly. "You're as stubborn as I was at your age."

"I'll take that as a compliment." She bent to kiss her aunt's cheek.

"We'll deal with the gossip somehow, I suppose." Her aunt tried one last volley.

"Darling, you know they'll gossip anyway. What I do or don't do won't change that."

"I suppose. It's just . . ." She caught Dinah's hand as she opened the door. "Be careful, Dinah. Please."

The intensity in her aunt's voice startled her. "Careful of what?"

"Marc. Just be wary of Marc. There may be more to his return than he's telling you."

Dinah could think of nothing to say to that. She slipped outside, closing the door quickly.

30

Aunt Kate, through some instinct, seemed to know more than she'd been told. Marcus did have an agenda, and it certainly wasn't one of which Aunt Kate would approve.

Well. Dinah stood on the piazza for a moment, pulling her jacket a little tighter around her. How had Aunt Kate stumbled upon that? Had she sensed something from Dinah's reaction?

She'd tried to hide her feelings after Marc had left the previous day. This idea of his that he'd look into Annabel's death — well, it might be understandable, but she couldn't help him. She had to make him see that.

She went out the brick walk to the gate in the wrought-iron fence that enclosed Aunt Kate's house and garden. The gate, like most of the others on the street, bore a wreath of magnolia leaves in honor of the season.

She touched the shining leaves. Maybe Court would like to make one, if he was determined to observe a real Charleston Christmas. Charlestonians were justifiably proud of their Christmas decor.

Crossing the quiet street, she had to will her steps not to lag. She took the step up to the curb, facing the gate in the wrought-iron fence. Marc's gate was similar to Aunt Kate's, but the black iron was worked into

31

the shape of a pineapple in the center —
the traditional symbol of Southern hospitality.

The house beyond, like Aunt Kate's and
most other old Charleston houses, was set
with its side to the street, facing the small
garden. According to local lore, the houses
were laid out that way because in the early
days of the city, home owners were taxed
based on how many windows faced the
street. The truth was probably that they'd
been clever enough to place the piazzas to
catch the breeze.

Open the gate, go up the brick walk. Her
breath came a little faster now. Ridiculous,
to hear her heart beating in her ears because
she neared her cousin's house. She should
have faced this long ago. If Aunt Kate
hadn't sent her away so quickly after the
tragedy —

She stopped herself. Aunt Kate had done
what she thought was best when confronted
with the death of one great-niece and the
emotional collapse of the other. She
couldn't be blamed.

Dinah had come back to Charleston as an
adult. She could have gone into the house
at any time, but she'd successfully avoided
every invitation.

Her first instinct had been right. Marc's

return would change all of them in ways she couldn't imagine.

She reached for the knocker and then paused. In the old days, she'd run in and out of Annabel's house as if it were her own. She shouldn't change things now. She grasped the brass knob, turned it and let the door swing open.

Please, help me do this. Slowly, she stepped inside.

The spacious center hallway stood empty, the renters' furniture gone with them. Weak winter sunshine through the stained-glass window on the landing cast oblongs of rose and green on the beige stair carpet. The graceful, winding staircase seemed to float upward.

The space was different, but the same. Even without Annabel's familiar furnishings, it echoed with her presence, as if at any moment she would sail through the double doors from the front parlor, silvery blond hair floating around her face, arms outstretched in welcome.

A shudder went through Dinah, and she took an involuntary step back.

"I know."

She turned. Marc stood in the doorway to the room that had once been his study. He'd exchanged the jacket and tie he'd worn the previous day for jeans and a casual ivory sweater. His eyes met hers gravely.

"I know," he said again. "I feel it, too. It's as if she's going to come through the door at any moment."

"Yes." She took a shaky breath, oddly reassured that his memories were doing the same thing to him. "I thought it would seem different to me, but it doesn't."

He moved toward her. "I thought I'd already done all my grieving." His voice roughened. "Then I found the grief was waiting here for me."

She nodded slowly. For the moment, the barriers between them didn't exist. Her throat was tight, but she forced the words out.

"I haven't been in here in ten years. I couldn't." Her voice shook a little. "Or maybe I was just a coward."

Marc grasped her shoulder in a brief, comforting touch and then took his hand away quickly, as if she might object.

"You're not a coward, Dinah. It's a natural reaction."

Ironic, that she'd just done what she'd told Aunt Kate not to do. Still, the confession of her weakness seemed to have eased the tension between them.

"What about Court? Is he having trouble

with being here?"

He shook his head. "He doesn't seem affected at all. It's unnerving, somehow."

It would be. She had a foolish urge to comfort Marc. "He was only three, after all. He slept through everything. He doesn't have the memories we do."

"No." He took a deep breath, his chest rising and falling. "I'm grateful for that."

"Maybe that makes it right that you kept him away from us." She couldn't help the bitterness that traced the words.

His jaw tightened. "I thought it was best for him."

"Obviously." Unexpected anger welled up in her. Both Marc and Aunt Kate had done what they thought was best, regardless of the consequences. "Are you sorry for the pain that caused us? Or do you just not care?"

Marc looked as startled as if a piece of furniture had suddenly railed at him. His dark eyes narrowed, and she braced for an attack.

Footsteps clattered down the stairs. They both jerked around toward the stairwell.

"Hey, Dad, can I go —"

The boy stopped at the sight of her, assessing her with a frank, open gaze. She did the same. Tall for thirteen — he had his father's height, but he hadn't broadened into it yet. He had Marc's dark eyes and hair, too, and for a moment she thought there was nothing of Annabel about him.

Then he trotted down the rest of the steps and came toward her, holding out his hand. "I know who you are." He smiled, and it was Annabel's smile, reaching out to clutch her heart.

"I know who you are, too." Her voice had gotten husky, but she couldn't help that. "Welcome home, Court."

Marc still couldn't get over how quickly Dinah had bonded with his son. He finished dusting the desk he and Court had carried from the attic to his study and put his laptop on it. That's where Dinah and Court were now, happily rummaging through the attic's contents to see what should be brought down for their use over the next few weeks.

At some point, he'd have to take a turn going through the attic. The thought of what that would entail made him cringe. He hadn't sorted a thing before he left Charleston. Now the reminders of his life with Annabel waited for him.

And, as Dinah had pointed out, he should make the house look furnished if he intended it to show well to prospective buyers. That hadn't occurred to him, and he could see already that Dinah would be invaluable to him. And to Court, apparently.

Court surely couldn't remember her. He'd only been three that summer. Still, Dinah had spent a lot of time with him. Maybe, at some level, Court sensed that they already had a relationship.

He opened his briefcase and stacked files next to the computer. The vacation time he'd taken to come here had been well earned, but it was impossible to walk away completely from ongoing cases. He'd have to spend part of each day in touch with the office if he expected to make this work.

His mind kept drifting back to that summer, unrolling images he hadn't looked at in years. Annabel hadn't felt well much of the time, and she'd been only too happy to turn Court over to Dinah. Face it, Annabel had been annoyed at being pregnant again, and each symptom had been a fresh excuse to snap at him about it.

He should have been more sympathetic, and he knew that painfully well now. He'd been absorbed in prosecuting a big case and relieved to escape the tension in the house by the need to work late most evenings.

What he hadn't expected was how devoted

Dinah became to Court, and how well she'd cared for him. Maybe she'd loved him so much because she'd always been alone, the only child being raised by an elderly aunt, shipped off to boarding school much of the time.

That was one thing he'd been determined not to do with Court. The boy had lost his mother, but his father had been a consistent presence in his life. He'd thought that was enough for Court, until the past few months.

"Are you stacking those files, or shredding them?" Dinah's voice startled him.

He glanced down at the files he'd unconsciously twisted in his hands. He put them down, smoothing the manila covers.

"I was thinking about something other than what I was doing. Where's Court?" He turned away from the desk, the sight of Dinah bringing an involuntary smile to his lips. "You have cobwebs in your hair."

She brushed at the mass of dark curls. "He found the boxes of Christmas ornaments, and he's busy going through them. Your attic needs some attention."

"That's just what I was thinking." He crossed to her, reaching out to pull the last wisp of cobweb from her hair. Her curls flowed through his fingers, silky and clinging. "I can't close on a sale until I clear the attic."

"I guess it has to be done." The shadow in her eyes said she knew how difficult that would be.

"Maybe you could help sort things out." There was probably every reason for her to say no to that. "There might be some things of Annabel's that you would like to keep as a remembrance. I'm sorry I didn't think of that sooner." He'd been too preoccupied with his own grief to pay sufficient heed to anyone else's.

She made a gesture that he interpreted as pushing that idea away with both hands. "I don't need anything to help me remember Annabel."

Once he'd been amused at how Dinah idolized his wife. Now he found himself wondering how healthy that had been.

"You might help me choose some things to keep for Court, then," he said smoothly. Court was probably a safe way to approach her. She'd been crazy about him when he was small, and he'd certainly returned the favor. "I remember him running down the hall full tilt, shouting 'Dinah, Dinah, Dinah.' "

A smile that was probably involuntary curved her lips. "I remember him singing

'Someone's in the Kitchen with Dinah.' You taught him that to tease me."

They were smiling at each other then, the image clear and bright between them. He leaned forward.

"You see, Dinah. We do have something in common."

Her eyes darkened. "If anything, too much." She took a breath, as if steadying herself. "Court really wants to have Christmas here."

He nodded. He was playing dirty pool, getting at her through Court, but he'd do what he had to. Any excuse to keep her in the house might help her remember.

"A Charleston Christmas with all the trimmings." He grimaced. "Thanks to the Internet, he has a calendar of every event through to First Night. If I try to skip a thing, he'll know it."

"Blame the tourist bureau for that." Her smile flickered. "They wouldn't want to miss a single visitor."

"Anyway —" He reached out, thinking to touch her hand, and then thought better of it. "Anyway, will you help me do Christmas, Dinah? For Court's sake?"

Aunt Kate had schooled her well. No one could tell from her expression the distaste she must feel, but somehow he knew it, bone deep.

"For Court's sake," she said. Then, cautioning, she added, "But we'll have to work around my job."

"You have a job?" He couldn't help the surprise in his tone.

"Of course I have a job." Her voice contained as much of an edge as she probably ever let show. "Did you think I sat around all day eating bonbons?"

"No. Sorry." He'd better not say that he'd assumed she'd been like Annabel, doing the round of society events and charity work until she married. "I am sorry. I guess I'm still thinking of you as a schoolgirl."

"I haven't been that in a long time." She seemed to accept the excuse, but those deep violet eyes were surprisingly hard to read.

"Sorry," he said again. "So, tell me what you do."

"I'm a forensic artist. I work for the Charleston Police Department primarily, but sometimes I'm called on by neighboring jurisdictions."

He couldn't have been more surprised if she'd said she was a lion tamer, but he suspected it wasn't a good idea to show that.

"That's —"

"Surprising? Appalling? Not a suitable job for a well brought up young lady?"

Her tone surprised him into a grin. "That sounds like what Aunt Kate might say."

"Among other things." Her face relaxed. "She still has trouble with it. She doesn't think I should be exposed to —" She stopped suddenly, her smile forgotten on her face.

"To violence," he finished for her. "It's too late for that, isn't it?"

"Yes. Much too late." It sounded like an epitaph.

If she let herself think about Marc's intentions for too long, Dinah could feel panic rising inside her. She'd forced herself to hold the subject at bay but now, driving to police headquarters the next day, she took a cautious look.

How could Marc possibly expect to learn anything new after ten years? Did he really think he could find the solution that had eluded the police?

Obviously, he did. In a sense, she could understand his determination. He saw a possible harm to Court in the unanswered questions, and he'd do anything for his son.

Ten years ago he'd loved his son, of course, but he'd been so preoccupied with his work that he hadn't been as available to Court as he should have been. Apparently, after he left Charleston, he'd turned his priorities around completely. She had to admire that.

But she wasn't so sure he was right about Court. Knowing more about his mother's life was admirable, but knowing more about his mother's death could only cause pain. She should know. She'd lived with that pain for too long.

What if Marc imagined she knew something about the night Annabel died that she'd never told? Everyone else had long since accepted the fact that she hadn't seen or heard anything. The dream was just that, a dream.

But Marc tended not to accept something just because everyone else did. She remembered that about him clearly. It had made him a good prosecutor. She wasn't sure it made him a safe friend.

She pulled into a parking place near the headquarters building on Lockwood Boulevard. Across the street, the black rectangular monument to fallen officers gleamed in the winter sunshine, making her heart clench. She pushed Marc into the back closet of her mind. She'd go inside, find Tracey, and concentrate on some complicated police case instead.

She hurried inside, clipping her identification to the pocket of the blazer she wore with tan slacks. She still smiled at the memory of Detective Tracey Elliott taking one look at her the first time they'd met and telling her not to come to headquarters again looking like a debutante.

At the time, Tracey had resented having a civilian artist foisted off on her by the chief of detectives, who'd been influenced in turn by an old friend of Aunt Kate's on the city council. Dinah had never regretted using influence to get in the door. She could prove her abilities only if they gave her a chance to try.

Nodding to several detectives who'd eventually accepted her, she wove through the maze of desks and file cabinets to where Tracey sat slumped over a thick sheaf of papers.

"Good morning."

Tracey shoved one hand through disheveled red curls, her green eyes warming with welcome. "Don't tell me it's good unless you've got some decent coffee stashed in that bag of yours."

It was a long-standing joke between them. Dinah set her tote bag on the desk and lifted out two foam cups, handing one to Tracey. She sat in the chair at the side of the gray metal desk and opened hers.

Tracey inhaled, seeming to gain energy just from the fragrant aroma. "You're my hero."

"Not quite. Just a hardworking forensic artist. Do you have something for me?"

She hoped. It had been a longer than usual time between assignments, and even though she didn't have to depend on her income from her work, that occasional paycheck gave her a sense of accomplishment, validating her professional status.

Her relationship with the department was still prickly. Some officers viewed any civilian on their turf with suspicion. The fact that she produced good results with difficult witnesses didn't necessarily change that.

"I'm not sure." Tracey frowned, shoving a manila folder over to her. "We have a witness to a knifing, but she's all over the place. We know she has to have seen something, but she's not admitting it."

Dinah scanned through the file, relieved to have something to think about besides Marc. "Is it gang-related?"

"Could be, but there's something about it that doesn't fit. The victim was a sixteen-year-old — parochial schoolkid, no gang involvement. The witness is her best friend. They were on their way home from a movie and took one shortcut too many."

She nodded, registering the site of the crime. It wasn't an area where she'd walk at night, alone or with a friend.

"Will the witness talk to me?"

"That's the problem." Tracey's expression spoke of her frustration. "Yesterday she would. That's why I called you. Today she says no. She knows nothing, saw nothing. And her friend won't be going to any more movies."

The words might have sounded flippant, but Dinah knew they weren't. She and the rough-edged detective had developed a friendship that probably surprised Tracey as much as it did her, and she knew the depth of pain that any death brought Tracey.

"I'm sorry." She wanted to say more, but knew she shouldn't cross that line. "Maybe she'll change her mind. Call me anytime."

Tracey nodded but gave her a probing look. "I thought you might be too busy since your cousin-in-law is back in town."

"How on earth did you hear about that?"

"He was a suspect in an unsolved murder. Word gets around, believe me."

"He didn't kill Annabel."

Tracey raised an eyebrow. "You sure of that?"

"Of course I am."

"Nice to be sure."

She swallowed irritation. "All right, Tracey. What's this all about? Did you get me down here to talk about Marc?"

"No." She shrugged. "But you're here. I couldn't help asking what you think about Marcus Devlin's return."

The irritation faded away. Tracey was just being Tracey. She couldn't blame her for that.

"I was surprised." That was honest. "I didn't think he'd ever want to come back, because of the tragedy."

"Why did he?"

"His house has been rented all these years. The renters recently moved out, so he came to make arrangements to put it on the market."

"A good Realtor could have taken care of that for him."

"You're like a dog with a bone, you know that?"

Tracey grinned. "That makes me a good detective. Why did he really come back?"

"Because of Court. His son. My cousin's son. Court wanted to see the house before it was sold. They're staying through the holidays. Not that it's police business."

"It's an open case," Tracey said gently. "Dinah, you must know that most often, a pregnant woman is killed by a husband or

47

boyfriend."

"Not even you can believe Marc would bring his thirteen-year-old son back to that house if he killed the boy's mother. Besides —" She stopped.

"Besides what?" Tracey prompted.

"Marc wants to find out the truth."

"I've heard that line before."

"Tracey, he didn't kill Annabel. He couldn't have."

"In that case, why does his return bother you so much?" Tracey held up her hand to stop a protest. "You're not that good at hiding your feelings."

"I was in the house that night," she said slowly. "I suppose you know that."

Tracey nodded. Of course she knew. She'd probably read all about the case before she'd ever agreed to work with Dinah.

"I don't want to have to relive the pain again. I loved Annabel. I want to protect her memory."

"Why does her memory need protecting?"

Dinah could only stare at Tracey, aghast that the words had come out of her mouth. She wasn't even conscious of thinking them, but now that she'd spoken, she knew it was true.

She wanted to protect Annabel's memory. And she didn't know why.

THREE

"We need to get a big tree, Dad. One that reaches the ceiling, okay?" Court leaned forward in the back seat of Marc's car, propping his arms on the back of Dinah's seat.

Marc didn't take his eyes off the road, but Dinah saw the slight smile that touched his lips. She thought she knew what he felt — that it was good to see Court enjoying himself so much.

She'd like to think so, too, but this tree-buying trip could turn out to be a disaster. She eyed Marc. Did he really not know what he could be walking into?

"How exactly do you expect to get a tree that big back to the house?" Marc asked, as if it were the only concern on his mind.

"We can tie it on top." Court twisted to look out the side window, bouncing Dinah's seat. "Hey, is that the water over there?"

"Charleston's a peninsula — we're practically surrounded by water. Your dad is taking us to the Christmas tree sale via the scenic route." As far as she was concerned, the longer it took to get there, the better. "Fort Sumter is there at the mouth of the harbor. We should take the boat trip out one day while you're here."

"Cool." Court pressed his face against the glass for a better look.

His absorption in the view gave her the opportunity for a carefully worded question aimed at Marc. "Are you sure you want to go to this particular tree sale?" she said quietly. "There are several others."

Marc's jaw tightened until it resembled a block of stone. "The Alpha Club sale still benefits charity, doesn't it?"

She nodded, not wanting to verbalize her concerns within Court's hearing.

"Then that's where we're going." Marc's tone didn't leave any room for argument.

Stubborn. He had always been stubborn, and that hadn't changed. He'd been a member of the Alpha Club once and active in the civic and charitable activities of the group of young professionals. They'd been fellow attorneys, fellow Citadel graduates, movers and shakers in Charleston society. Did Marc think he'd find a welcome there now?

Her stomach clenched. She wanted to

protect both him and Court from any unpleasantness, but she could hardly do that if he insisted on walking right into the lion's den.

Protect. She'd told Tracey she wanted to protect Annabel's memory. The truth probably was that she couldn't protect any of them, including herself.

Fortunately, or perhaps unfortunately, they drew up then at the parking lot that had been transformed into a Christmas tree paradise — decorated trees, garlands, lights, live trees, cut trees, trees of every shape and size. The Alpha Club did its sale in style.

"Wow." That seemed to be Court's favorite expression. He slid out of the car as soon as it stopped. "I'll find just the right one." He loped into a forest of cut trees, disappearing from sight.

Dinah got out more slowly and waited while Marc came around the car to join her. "He definitely hasn't lost his enthusiasm, has he?"

"Not at all." His smile was automatic, and she thought some other concern lay behind it. "He was asking me questions today about your family history," he said abruptly. "I tried to answer him, but I'm probably not the best source for Westlake family history."

She knew what he was looking for. "Aunt

Kate is." Aunt Kate was the repository of family stories that would be lost when she was gone unless someone cared enough to hear and remember them.

"I know she doesn't want to see me." The words were clipped. "Do you think she'd talk to Court about the family?"

She could only be honest. "I don't know. I'll ask her."

"Thanks, Dinah. I appreciate it."

His hand wrapped around hers in a gesture of thanks. It lasted just for an instant. It shouldn't mean anything. It didn't mean anything. So why did she feel as if the touch surged straight to her heart?

It was nothing. A hangover from the teenage crush she'd had once. She took a breath, inhaling the crisp scents of pine and fir, and shoved her hands in her jacket pockets.

"We'd better find Court, before he picks out a twenty-foot tree."

They moved into the mass of trees. And mass of people, too. It seemed half of Charleston had chosen this evening to search for the perfect tree. Surely, in this crowd, it would be possible to find a tree and leave without encountering any of Marc's one-time friends.

They rounded a corner of the makeshift

aisle through the tree display, and she saw that she'd been indulging in a futile hope. Court, pointing at a huge fir, was deep in conversation with a salesman. The man didn't need to turn for her to recognize him. And judging by the quick inhalation Marc gave, he knew him instantly as well.

He hesitated, and then he strode forward, holding out his hand. "Phillips. You're just the person I was hoping to see."

Phillips Carmody turned, peering gravely through the glasses that were such a part of his persona that Dinah couldn't imagine him without them. Then his lean face lit with a smile.

"Marc." He clasped Marc's hand eagerly. "How good to see you. It's been too long."

"It wouldn't have been so long if you'd come to Boston to see us."

So Phillips had been welcome to visit, while Annabel's family had not. Anger pricked her, and she forced it away as she approached the two men and Court, who looked on curiously, the tree forgotten for the moment.

"Phillips can't leave Charleston," she said. "The city's history would collapse without him."

She tilted her face up to receive Phillips's customary peck on the cheek. He always seemed to hesitate, as if remembering that it was no longer appropriate to pat her on the head.

"Dinah, dear, you're here, too." He focused on Court. "And so you must be Courtney. Annabel's son." His voice softened on the words. "I'm Phillips Carmody, one of your father's oldest friends."

Court shook hands. "I'm happy to meet you, sir." He gave the smile that was so like Annabel's, and she thought Phillips started a bit. It came as a shock to him, probably, as it had to her.

"How long are you staying?" Phillips glanced at Marc. "I heard you were putting the house on the market."

"I see the grapevine is still active." Marc seemed to relax in Phillips's company, his smile coming more easily now.

Dinah felt some of her tension dissipate as the men talked easily. It looked as if her fears had been foolish.

Marc had handed over a shocking amount of money and they'd negotiated when the tree would be delivered when the interruption came.

"Phillips! What are you doing?"

Dinah didn't have to turn to know who was there. Margo Carmody had an unmistakable voice — sugar-coated acid, Annabel

54

had always said. How someone as sweet as Phillips ended up married to a woman like that was one of life's mysteries.

Dinah pinned a smile to her face and turned. "Hello, Margo. Are you working the sale as well?"

Margo ignored her, the breach in etiquette announcing how upset she was. Margo never ignored the niceties of polite society. Except, apparently, when confronted by a man her acid tongue had proclaimed a murderer.

"Look who's here, my dear." Nervousness threaded Phillips's voice. "It's Marcus. And his son, Courtney."

Margo managed to avoid eye contact with both of them. "You're needed back at the cash desk, Phillips. Come along, now." She turned and stalked away, leaving an awkward silence behind.

"I'm sorry." Faint color stained Phillips's cheeks. "I'm afraid I must go. Perhaps I'll see you again while you're here. It was nice to meet you, Court." He scuttled away before Dinah could give in to the temptation to shake him.

"That woman gets more obnoxious every year." She could only hope Court would believe Margo's actions were motivated by general rudeness and not aimed at them.

"How Phillips stands her, I don't know."

"He seems to come to heel when she snaps her fingers." Marc's dry tone was probably intended to hide the pain he must feel.

"Would you expect anything else?" The voice came from behind her.

Dinah turned. Not James Harwood. It was really too much that they'd run into both of the men who'd been Marc's closest friends in the same night. Still, James and Phillips ran in identical social circles, and they were both mainstays of the Alpha Club, regulars at the elegant old building that graced a corner of Market Street near The Battery.

"Hello, James." This time Marc didn't bother to offer his hand. It was clear from the coldness on James's face that it wouldn't be taken.

"James, I —" A lady always smoothes over awkward situations. That was one of Aunt Kate's favorite maxims, but Dinah couldn't think of a thing to say.

"You shouldn't have come back." James bit off the words. "You're not welcome here."

Court took a step closer to his father. The hurt in his eyes cut Dinah to the heart. Court shouldn't have to hear things like that. Marc should have realized what might happen when he brought him here.

"I'm sorry you feel that way." Marc's tone was cool, the voice of a man meeting rudeness with calm courtesy. But a muscle in his jaw twitched as if he'd like to hit something. Or someone.

"I think we're ready to leave now." She'd better intervene before they both forgot themselves. "We have what we came for, don't we, Court?"

Politeness required that Court turn to her, and she linked her arm with his casually. "Ready, Marc?"

Please. Don't make matters worse by getting into a quarrel with James. It's not worth it.

Whether he sensed her plea or not, she didn't know. He flexed his hands, and she held her breath. Then he turned and walked steadily toward the car.

"Hey, wouldn't it look cool if we strung lights along the banister?" Court, standing halfway up the staircase, looked down.

Struck by a sudden flicker of resemblance to Annabel in his son's face, Marc couldn't answer for a moment. Then he managed a smile.

"Sounds great. What do you think?"

He turned to Dinah, who was dusting off

the stack of ornament boxes they'd just carried down from the attic. In jeans and a faded College of Charleston sweatshirt, her dark curls pulled back in a loose ponytail, she looked little older than the sixteen-year-old he remembered.

She straightened, frowning at the stairwell. "What do you think of twining lights with an evergreen swag along the railing? I think I remember several swags in a plastic bag in the attic."

"I'll go see." Court galloped up the steps, managing to raise a few stray dust motes that danced in the late-afternoon light. A thud announced that he'd arrived at the attic door.

Marc winced. "Sorry. Court doesn't do much of anything quietly."

"I'd be worried about him if he did." Dinah glanced up the stairwell, as if following Court in her mind's eye. "At least he's not showing any signs that being here bothers him. And if he's not upset after what happened last night —"

"I know. I guess I haven't said you were right, but you were. We should have gone somewhere else for the tree."

"I wish I hadn't been right." Her face was warm with sympathy.

Maybe it was the sympathy that led him

to say more than he intended. "I expected antagonism from Margo. She never liked Phil's friendship with me, and she and Annabel were like oil and water."

"I remember." Dinah's smile flickered. "Annabel had a few uncomplimentary names for her."

"Which she shouldn't have said in front of you." He ran a hand through his hair. "Margo doesn't matter. But Phil and James —"

He stopped. No use going over it again. No use remembering when the three of them had been the three musketeers, back in their Citadel days. He'd thought the bonds they'd formed then were strong enough to survive anything. Obviously he'd been wrong.

"Phillips is still your friend. He's just not brave enough to stand up to Margo. He never has been."

"Maybe." He'd grant her Phil, and his patent knuckling under to the woman he'd married. But . . . "James thinks I killed Annabel." He checked the stairwell, but Court was still safely out of hearing, rummaging in the attic.

Dinah started to say something. Then she closed her mouth. It didn't matter. Her expressive face said it for her.

"You think I should have been prepared for that. You tried to warn me."

"I thought it might be awkward. I didn't expect outright rudeness."

She sounded as primly shocked as Aunt Kate might have, and he couldn't suppress a smile.

"You don't need to laugh at me," she said tartly. "They were all brought up to know better."

"Next you'll say that their mothers would be ashamed of them."

"Well, they would." She snapped the words, but her lips twitched a little. "Oh, all right. We're hopelessly old-fashioned here. I suppose James has been in politics too long to have much sense left. And besides, you know how he felt about Annabel."

That startled him. "Do I?"

She blinked. "Everyone knows he was crazy about her."

"I didn't." Had he been hopelessly stupid about his own wife? "How did Annabel feel about him?"

"Oh, Marc." Dinah's eyes filled with dismay. "Don't think that. It never meant anything. Just a crush on his part."

"And Annabel?" Dinah wanted him to let it go, but he couldn't.

"Annabel never had eyes for anyone but

you. She just — I think she was flattered by James's attention. That was all. Honestly."

She looked so upset at having told him that he didn't have the heart to ask anything else. But he filed it away for further thought.

He bent to pick up the stack of boxes. "We may as well take these to the family room. If I know my son, he'll drag everything out, but he won't be as good about putting things away."

Dinah went ahead of him to open the door to what would be the back parlor in most Charleston homes. They'd always used it as a family room, and he and Court had managed to bring down most of the furniture that belonged here. By tacit agreement, they'd avoided the front parlor, the room where Annabel died.

"Court looks so much like you. Looking at him must be like looking at a photo of you at that age."

He set the boxes down on the wooden coffee table that had been a barn door before an enterprising Charleston artisan had transformed it. "Funny. I was thinking that I saw a little of Annabel in his face when he looked down from the stairs."

"I know." Her voice softened, and he realized he hadn't done a good enough job of hiding his feelings. "I see it, too — just certain flashes of expression."

He sank onto the brown leather couch and frowned absently at the tree they'd set up in the corner. He'd told Court it would be too big for the room. The top brushed the ceiling, and he'd have to trim it before the treetop angel would fit.

"Maybe it's because we're back here. My memory of Annabel had become a kind of still photo, and she was never that."

"No, she wasn't." Dinah perched on the coffee table, her heart-shaped face pensive. "I've never known anyone as full of life as she was. Maybe that's why I admired her. She was so fearless, while I —" She grimaced. "I always was such a chicken."

"Don't say that about yourself." He leaned forward almost involuntarily to touch her hand. "You've been through some very bad times and come out strong and whole. That's something to be proud of."

"I'm not so sure about that, but thank you."

For a moment they were motionless. It was dusk outside already, and he could see their reflections in the glass of the French door, superimposed on the shadowy garden.

He leaned back, not wanting to push too hard. "Being back in the house again — has it made you think any more about what happened?"

"No." The negative came sharp and quick, and she crossed her arms, as if to protect herself. "I don't remember anything about that night."

"That summer, then. There might have been something you noticed that I didn't."

She shook her head. "Do you think I didn't go over it a thousand times in my mind? There was nothing."

And if there was, he suspected it was buried too deeply to be reached willingly. Dinah had protected herself the only way she could.

He'd try another tack. "You're connected with the police. If there's any inside information floating around, people might be more willing to talk to you than to me."

Dinah stared at him, eyes huge. "Someone already talked to me. About you."

"Who?" Whatever had been said clearly had upset her.

"A detective I work with."

He was going to have to drag the words out of her. "What did he say?"

"She. She said . . ."

He could see the movement of her neck as she swallowed.

"She reminded me that the case is still open. And that you're still a suspect."

He should have realized. He, of all people, knew how the police mind-set worked. And this detective, whoever she was, wanted to protect one of their own. Wanted to warn her off, probably, too.

"Dinah, I'm sorry."

"For what?"

"I didn't think. I've put you in an untenable position. I shouldn't have. If you want to back off . . ." He shook his head. "Of course you do. I'll make some excuse to Court."

As if he'd heard his name, Court came into the room, arms filled with evergreen swags. "I found them," he announced happily. "But we don't have nearly enough lights, Dad. We need to go get some more before we can do this. Want to come, Dinah?"

She stood, smiling at Court. "You two go." She glanced at Marc, the smile stiffening a little. "I'll unpack the ornaments while you're out. I'll be here when you get back."

He understood the implication. She wasn't going to run out on them, although she had every reason to do so. He felt a wave of relief that was ridiculously inappropriate.

"Thank you, Dinah."

Was she crazy? Dinah listened as the front

64

door clicked shut behind Marc and Court. Marc had understood. Or at least he'd understood the spot he'd put her in professionally, if not personally. He'd given her the perfect out, and she hadn't taken it.

She couldn't. She may as well face that fact, at least. No matter how much she might want to stay away from Marc and all the bitter reminders, too many factors combined to force her to stay.

She'd been thirteen when he married Annabel, the same age Court was now. With no particular reason to, he'd been kind to her, putting up with her presence when he'd probably have preferred to be alone with his bride, inviting her to the beach house at Sullivan's Island, even teaching her to play tennis. She'd told herself she didn't owe Marc anything, but she did.

And Annabel — how much more she owed Annabel, her bright, beautiful cousin. She'd loved her with a passion that might otherwise have been expended on parents, siblings, cousins her own age. Since she didn't have any of them, it all went to Annabel.

Finally there was Court. Her lips curved in a smile, and she bent to take the cover off the first box of ornaments. Court had stolen her heart again, just as he had the first time she'd seen him staring at her with unfocused infant eyes when he was a few days old.

Whatever it cost her, she couldn't walk away from this. All her instincts told her Marc was wrong in what he wanted to do, but she couldn't walk away.

She began unpacking the boxes, setting the ornaments on the drop-leaf table near the tree. They were an odd mix — some spare, sophisticated glass balls that Annabel had bought, but lots of delicate, old-fashioned ornaments that had been in the family for generations.

One tissue-wrapped orb felt heavy in her hand, and an odd sense of recognition went through her. She knew what it was even before she unwrapped it — an old, green glass fisherman's weight that she'd found in an antique shop on King Street and given to Annabel for Christmas the year before she died.

For a moment she held the glass globe in her hand. The lamplight, falling on it, reflected a distorted image of her own face, and the glass felt warm against her palm. She was smiling, she realized, but there were tears in her eyes.

She set the ball carefully on the table. She'd tell Court about the ornaments, including that one. That kind of history was what he needed from this Christmas in Charleston.

She'd been working in silence, with only an occasional crackle from a log in the fireplace for company, when she heard a thud somewhere in the house. She paused, her hand tightening on a delicate shell ornament. They hadn't come back already, had they?

A few quiet steps took her to the hallway. Only one light burned there, and the shadows had crept in, unnoticed. She stood still, hearing nothing but the beat of her own heart.

Then it came again, a faint, distant creaking this time. She'd lived in old houses all her life. They had their own language of creaks and groans as they settled. That had to be what she'd heard.

She listened another moment. Nothing. She was letting her nerves get the better of her at being alone in the house.

A shrill sound broke the silence, and she started, heart hammering. Then, realizing what it was, she shook her head at her own foolishness and went in search of her cell phone, its ring drowning out any other noise. Marc hadn't had the phone service started. She'd given him her cell-phone number in case he needed to reach her.

The phone was in the bottom of her bag, which she finally found behind the sofa in the family room. She snatched it up and pressed the button.

"Hello?" Her voice came out oddly breathless.

"Dinah? You sound as if you've been running. Listen, do you think a string of a hundred white lights is enough? Court put two strings in the cart when I wasn't looking."

Her laugh was a little shaky. "You may as well get two. If you don't use the second one, you can always take it back."

"I guess you're right." She heard him say something distantly, apparently to the cashier. Then his voice came back, warm and strong in her ear. "Is everything all right? You don't sound quite yourself."

"It's nothing. Really. I was just scaring myself, thinking I heard someone in the house." When she said the words, she realized that was what she'd been thinking at some deep level. Someone in the house.

"Get out. Now." The demand was sharp and fast as the crack of a whip.

"I'm sure I just imagined —"

"Dinah, don't argue. Just get out. And don't hang up. Keep talking to me."

Logic told her he was panicking unnecessarily, probably visited by the terrible memory of coming into the house and finding Annabel. But even if he was, his panic was contagious.

Holding the phone clutched tightly against her ear, she raced across the room, through the hallway and plunged out the door.

FOUR

Dinah slid back on the leather couch in the family room, cradling a mug of hot chocolate between her palms, and looked at Court. He'd collapsed on the couch next to her into that oddly boneless slouch achieved only, as far as she could tell, by adolescent boys. His mug was balanced precariously on his stomach.

"More cocoa?"

He shook his head, the mug wavering at the movement. "I'm okay." He watched her from under lowered lids. "How about you? You feeling okay? Anything you want?"

He was attempting to take care of her, obviously. The thought sent a rush of tenderness through her. She tried to keep the feeling from showing in her face. He wouldn't appreciate that when he was trying so hard to be nonchalant about the prospect of an intruder in the house.

Marc's footsteps sounded, far above them.

He was searching the attic, probably. She was convinced he wouldn't find anything. She'd simply overreacted to being in the house alone, and, in turn, he'd overreacted. There'd been no one in the house.

It was probably best not to talk to Court about that. She nodded toward the bare tree, propped in its stand in the corner. "Do you always have a big tree at home?"

The corner of his mouth twitched, making him look very like his father. "Not big enough. We have a town house. It's plenty big enough for the two of us, but Dad always says there's not room for a big tree." He sent a satisfied glance toward the tree. "This is more like it."

"Aunt Kate — well, I guess she's actually your great-grand-aunt — hasn't had a real tree since I grew up. She's content with a little artificial one on a table."

Court's great-grand-aunt. Aunt Kate had to be made to see that she must talk with Court about his ancestors. She didn't have to discuss his mother, if she didn't want to, but she couldn't deny a relationship with the boy.

"Yeah, that's what my grandma and granddad do, too. They say real trees are too expensive in Arizona, anyway."

"Do you see them much?" Marc's parents

had left Charleston within a year of Annabel's death, moving to Arizona supposedly for his mother's health. It might have been that, of course, but she doubted it. Did they feel they were living in exile?

"We were out for Thanksgiving." Court maneuvered himself upright, letting the mug tip nearly to the point of no return before grasping it. "Maybe I should go see if Dad needs any help."

"I don't think —"

"Dad doesn't." Marc came in on the words. "Everything's fine."

Dinah sensed some reservation behind the words, and her stomach tightened. There was something he didn't want to say in front of Court.

"You sure? I could check the cellar." Court obviously considered that he should have been included in the search.

"Already done." Marc glanced at his watch. "If you want to e-mail your buddies before we call it a night, you'd better go do it."

"How about the tree? I thought we were going to decorate."

"Tomorrow's time enough for that. Dinah has to go home."

"Okay, okay," he grumbled, but went toward the door. "You'll help tomorrow, won't you, Dinah?"

She was absurdly pleased that he wanted her. "I have to go into work in the morning, but I'll come and help in the afternoon."

Court lifted an eyebrow in Marc's characteristic expression. "I wouldn't mind seeing police headquarters, you know."

"Dinah's going to work, not giving tours." Marc gave him a gentle shove. "Go on, and don't stay online too late. I'm walking Dinah home."

Court disappeared across the hall, raising his hand in a quick goodbye. Dinah waited until the office door closed behind him.

"Did you find anything?"

"Nothing to take to the police." His level brows drew down. "Anyone could have popped the back door with a screwdriver, though. I blocked it tonight with a two by four, but I'll put a new lock on tomorrow." He picked up her jacket, holding it for her. "Come on. I'll walk you home."

"That's not necessary." She slid her arms into the jacket. He adjusted it and then clasped her shoulders.

"Maybe not, but I'm going to."

The sense of being protected and taken care of was entirely too tempting. But she wasn't the little cousin any longer. She was a big girl now. She took a deliberate step away, putting some space between them.

"You're overreacting. All that was wrong was a creaking old house and my overactive imagination. There was no need for you to come rushing back here like a . . . a super-hero, out to rescue the damsel in distress."

"Is that what I did?" His face had gone still.

"Yes." Marc had to understand that their relationship had changed. They were never going back to the way things had been between them. "I didn't need rescuing."

He frowned at her for a long moment. Then he seemed to come to a decision. He pulled something from his pocket and held it out to her.

"Probably you're right. But I didn't feel like taking it for granted after reading that."

She smoothed out the crumpled sheet of yellow tablet paper. The message on it was printed in pencil, in block letters. It informed Marc, with the embellishment of considerable profanity, that he was a killer and that he would be punished.

She resisted the urge to drop it and scrub her hands. "Where did you get it?"

"It was shoved in the mailbox sometime today. Luckily I found it, not Court."

"In the mailbox — not mailed?"

"No." His expression became grimmer, if

that was possible. "That means the author of that missive was on my veranda today. If I overreacted when you thought someone was in the house, I had good reason."

"I guess I would have, too. But people who write anonymous notes don't usually act on them."

"Is that the police consultant speaking?" He shook his head, taking the paper back and tucking it into his pocket. "Sorry. I know you mean well. I know what you say is true. But it's not easy to be rational when —"

She knew what he was going to say. "When someone you love has been killed in this house."

He gave her a baffled, angry look. "Exactly. Irrational or not, that's what I felt. And maybe it's not so irrational. The person who killed Annabel is still out there, remember?"

"I'm not likely to forget. But if he has any brains at all, he'll stay as far away from you as possible."

"Maybe so. Still, I'm not taking any chances. So tomorrow I'll put a new lock on the back door. And tonight I'll walk you home."

There was more that she wanted to say, but she didn't think he was in the mood to hear it. So she went ahead of him to the front door, stepping out onto the piazza where she'd fled so precipitously earlier, listening to him lock the door carefully.

The air was chilly, and she stuffed her hands into her pockets. A full moon rode low in the sky, sending spidery shadows across the walk. She heard Marc's footsteps behind her, and he reached out to push the gate open when she reached it.

She paused on the walk. "You could just watch me to my door, you know."

"I could. But I'm not going to." He slid his hand into the crook of her arm.

The street was still and deserted. She glanced up at him as they crossed. "Are you sure you want to stay, after all this?"

"Court would never agree to leave now. And I keep my promises to my son. Besides —"

He paused, and she couldn't make out his expression in the moonlight.

"Besides?"

He shrugged. "I told you. Now that I'm here, I know I can't go back to being content with the status quo." His fingers tightened on her arm, and she felt his determination through their pressure. "Do you know why I went into a private firm when we moved away?"

The change of subject bewildered her. "Well, I suppose I thought you wanted a change. Or to make more than you could as a prosecutor."

"There's certainly that." There was a certain grim humor to his tone. "I've done far better financially. But that's not why. I went into a firm because no prosecutor's office or state's attorney's office would have me. Not with the shadow of my wife's murder hanging over me."

The bitterness in his tone forbade any facile answer. For a moment she couldn't say anything at all.

"I'm sorry," she said finally. "I didn't realize. I should have." She hesitated, feeling her way. "I guess I've continued to look at what happened then as if I were still sixteen."

"You're not sixteen anymore." They'd reached the gate, and he opened it for her. "Now you can face what happened as an adult."

Marc sounded very sure of that, and he didn't seem to expect a response. That was just as well, because she wasn't sure she could give one.

"Good night, Marc."

He nodded. "Sleep well."

She doubted that. She very much doubted it.

Marc wasn't sure how long it had been since he'd seen his son so thoroughly happy, so completely unclouded. Since before he'd started asking questions about his mother, probably.

"But Dad —" Court hung over the stair railing, looking ready to take flight. "Some colored lights along the porch would look really cool."

"Piazza, not porch." Nobody had a piazza in Boston, and the old Charleston term had come back to him.

"Piazza, then. We could get the kind that blink."

Much as he liked seeing Court happy, he had to draw the line somewhere. The decorating was getting out of hand.

"I'm afraid not." Dinah intervened before he could come up with a way to nix blinking lights. "There are regulations on the types of decorations you can have on houses in the historic district. No blinking lights." She smiled up at Court from where she sat on the floor, attaching the bottom of the garland around the newel post. "There should be a crèche somewhere in the attic.

It was your mother's when she was a little girl."

That was all Court needed to hear. "Good deal." He galloped up the stairs.

"Thanks, Dinah." He hooked the garland on the small nail under the railing. "I don't know what he'd have come up with next."

"Reindeer on the roof, probably." She smiled, but her eyes seemed shadowed, somehow. She turned away, as if she felt his gaze, dark hair sweeping down to hide her face.

"Probably," he agreed. He focused on the garland. "Is it bothering you? Being here?"

"Not at all." The response came too quickly.

"Something's wrong." He leaned his elbow on the newel post, looking down at her. "Can't you tell me what?"

She stretched, slim shoulders moving under the deep purple sweater she wore. "It's work. You wouldn't be interested."

"I would definitely be interested," he said. "Come on, talk." He still had trouble picturing Dinah in a police setting. A cotillion, yes. Police headquarters, no.

"Tracey Elliott is a detective who often calls on me. She's working a case where a young girl was killed. The only witness is her friend, a girl only a couple of years older than Court." She shook her head. "I have to struggle for my detachment every time I'm called in, but this one —" She shrugged expressively. "It's hard."

"Can't someone else take this case?" The instinct he had to protect her was probably ridiculous. She wouldn't thank him for it.

She stiffened. "It's my job. I don't want anyone else to take it. Besides, it's going to sound conceited, but I can do this if anyone can. She'd shut down completely for a uniformed officer with a computer identification kit."

"I guess I can see that." Naturally a scared, traumatized teenager would rather talk to someone like Dinah. "Are you getting anywhere with her?"

"She keeps backing away, insisting she didn't see anything. But the evidence shows that she had to have witnessed the crime. So we keep trying. She's agreed to see me again tomorrow morning."

"And that makes you tense." He was still trying to get at the cause for the shadow in her eyes.

"Doing it is hard. But it's worth it if I get something that leads them to a killer, don't you think?"

She looked up at him, dark curls flowing away from her heart-shaped face, and he was struck by several feelings at once. That Dinah had grown into a woman to admire, doing something important, and that he was stuck in a job that, however rewarding financially, didn't measure up to his dreams.

"Yes, I guess it is."

Dinah stood, her hands full of strings of lights. "We'd better get on with this, or Court will think we're not doing our share."

He went onto the first step. "Just feed the lights up to me, and I'll attach them. By the way, I almost forgot to tell you. Remember Glory Morgan?"

"Of course. She was your housekeeper. I run into her once in a while."

"She's agreed to come in and work a few days a week while we're here. I thought that would be a help in getting the house ready to sell."

"I see." Her brows arched. "Are you sure that's your only reason?"

She was entirely too quick. "You know, there's something to be said for not jumping to conclusions."

"I'm a grown-up now, remember? You're hoping that having Glory here will somehow help you. But if Glory knew anything, she'd have talked long ago. She's as honest and forthright as they come."

"She'd have told anything she knew about

Annabel's death. I'm hoping there may be something else, something that happened that summer that will give me a lead. The police would have found anything obvious. I'm looking for something that's not obvious."

Dinah nodded. "I guess I understand, but I'm not sure anything will come of it. Still, it'll be worth having Glory here just to taste her corn bread again."

"She'll give Court a taste of some real Charleston cooking, that's for sure. Maybe I ought to look up the yardman, too. I don't suppose you remember him. Jasper Carr."

"I remember him. Annabel didn't like him."

For an instant it didn't register. Then he looked down at her. She was busy with the lights, and she'd spoken almost absently.

Careful. Don't scare the memory away.

"What makes you say that she didn't like him?"

Apparently he hadn't been casual enough with the question, because Dinah looked up, her eyes wide. "I don't know. I don't know why I said that."

Don't rush her. "You must have noticed something Annabel said or did that showed you she didn't like him."

He tried to say it easily, not to let too

much interest show in his voice. This was what he'd hoped, that Dinah would remember something no one else had noticed about that summer.

She sat back on her heels, the lights forgotten in her lap. Her dark eyes seemed to be looking far away. No, far inward would be more accurate.

"Annabel came in from the garden. She'd gone out to pick some flowers for the table. She said something like, 'That Carr. Marc should get rid of him. I don't like the way he sneaks around.' " She blinked, then focused on him. "Didn't she ever tell you that?"

"Not that I can remember."

"Well, maybe she didn't want to bother you. You had that big case going on and you were out most of the time."

He'd been out most of the time. Dinah said it in a matter-of-fact way. She wasn't accusing him.

But he accused himself. He hadn't been there. He'd been too wrapped up in his work to notice what was happening in his own house.

"Marc, what's wrong?" Dinah stood, her hand on the banister. "Do you think Carr had something to do with Annabel's death?"

"He wasn't the person I was thinking of. I

don't think the police paid much attention to him. There didn't seem any reason to."

"The fact that Annabel didn't like him isn't a reason for murder."

"No, it's not. But that may not be all there was to it. She didn't say anything else about him to you?"

Dinah shook her head. "What are you going to do?"

"I think I'll have a talk with Glory about Carr. Annabel may have said something to her." He put his hand over hers on the railing. "Thanks, Dinah. You've given me something to look into, at any rate."

She was frowning. "What did you mean when you said Carr wasn't the person you were thinking of?"

He hadn't intended to tell her, but maybe she had the right to know. He'd already involved her more than he'd intended. "There was someone else. Someone I'd prosecuted who'd made threats. His name was Leonard Hassert."

"But if you prosecuted him, wasn't he in prison?"

"He should have been. They let him out early — good behavior, so they said." Bitterness rose like bile. Hassert shouldn't have been running around loose.

"Surely the police investigated him."

"They checked him out. He had an alibi. Three people were prepared to swear he couldn't have been anywhere near here that night."

"But if so —"

"People do lie, Dinah." His tone was gently mocking. "I'm not satisfied, even if the police were. I think it all bears looking at again."

"I suppose so." Her hand closed on his. "But —"

"Hey, aren't you done with those lights yet?" Court's voice sounded from above them. Marc looked up, to see his son hanging over the railing.

"We're working on it."

Dinah snatched her hand free. "Do you think we've been loafing? We'll be finished in a jiffy. I'll take the lights up to the top and work my way down."

She darted past him up the stairs. Uneasiness moved through him at the sight.

"You don't need to . . ." he began.

Dinah turned, the string of lights in her hand. The smile ebbed from her face, like sand washed by the outgoing tide. She looked down, toward the hall, her fair skin paling. She grabbed the railing.

He reached her in a millisecond. He hadn't thought. He'd been stupid. "Dinah, are you all right?"

She took a breath and straightened, her hand falling away from the railing. "I'm fine." Her gaze evaded his. "Let's get this finished."

"Right. We will." He took the string of lights from her. "You go down and tell me if I'm getting them even, okay?" It was the only thing he could think of to get her off the stairs without Court noticing anything.

She nodded and went on down the steps. It must have taken an effort not to hurry.

He wanted her to remember. But in his need to know, he hadn't thought about what remembering might do to Dinah.

FIVE

Dinah sat bolt upright in bed, a cry strangled in her throat. She clapped her hand over her mouth. Had she actually cried out, or had it been only in the dream?

No, not dream. Nightmare. Shivering, she clutched the quilt around her. She was cold and perspiring at the same time, her heart still pounding with remembered fear.

Breathe in, breathe out. Concentrate on your breath, let your pulse slow, your heartbeat steady. How could a mere dream, a product of the mind, produce such violent physical symptoms? She couldn't have been more terrified if she'd been in actual danger.

She drew her knees up and wrapped her arms around them. The soft, much-washed cotton of the quilt was as soothing as her mother's caress. She was all right. She was safe in the room that had been hers since she'd come to live with Aunt Kate when she was nine. The double-wedding-ring quilt had been her mother's; the sleigh bed had been her father's.

She looked automatically toward the bedside table. It was too dark to make out their features in the silver-framed photograph, but she didn't need the light. She knew how they looked — always young, always laughing, always holding each other — the way they'd looked before Hurricane Hugo tore apart all their lives.

She plucked the robe she'd left across the bottom of the bed, pulling it around her as she slid from the cocoon of covers. Her toes curled into the hooked rug that lay over the polished heart of pine floor, the touch grounding her.

She was all right. She wasn't trapped in the dream, standing on the staircase in Marc and Annabel's house, looking down at the dimly lit hallway. Seeing the sliver of light from the front parlor, hearing angry voices, being afraid without knowing why.

A shudder went through her, and she gritted her teeth until it faded. She always woke from the dream at that moment. She never saw the rest of it, but maybe that was God's providence, protecting her from something too terrible to be borne.

She knew how the story ended, in any event. It ended with Annabel, her beautiful cousin Annabel, dead on the floor in front of the Adam fireplace in her elegant parlor.

She took another long, shaky breath and crossed the room. Her eyes were growing accustomed to the dimness, touching one familiar object after another. Aunt Kate had created this space for her when she took Dinah in, seeming happy to trade the peace and comfort of an elderly spinster's quiet existence for the trials of raising a distraught, grief-stricken child.

Reaching the window, Dinah slid down to her knees, pushing up the sash so that she could prop her elbows on the low, wide sill. The chill night air touched her face. The quiet, dark street slept. She was twenty-six, not sixteen, and she wasn't afraid.

Marc's house slept, too. For ten years it had been rented to a busy professional couple whose brisk lives and genteel parties had routed any shadows left from the tragedy that happened there. Still, despite repeated invitations, she'd avoided going inside. She'd thought she'd been doing the right thing, dealing with her grief in her own way. Instead she'd just been delaying the inevitable.

It didn't take too much effort to figure out what had brought on the nightmare tonight. That moment when she'd run heedlessly up the stairs and then turned —

Her heart was thudding again, and she took another deep breath, forcing herself to be calm. She would not relive that moment, staring down at the hallway, feeling her vision darken as her ten-years-younger self filled her mind.

Marc had known, of course. She couldn't miss the pity in his face when he'd reached her, made an excuse to get her off the stairs.

A little flare of anger went through her. Why should he pity her? It was his idea, after all. He wanted her to remember.

I can't remember, Father. I don't know anything. Why can't he understand that?

If I did know anything —

Her mind backed away from that thought. She didn't. She didn't.

She covered her face with her palms. Even in prayer, she couldn't go that deeply.

You know. She pressed down the welling tide of panic. *You understand, Father. This is how I cope. Isn't it going to be enough?*

Maybe not.

She rose slowly, stretching cramped muscles. From the bedroom alcove, a light blinked on her computer. Copies of the forensic drawings she'd done were stacked neatly on her desk, next to the case with her sketching materials, ready to go at a moment's notice.

Ironic, wasn't it? Her sketches had helped crime victims deal with their traumatic memories, but she could do nothing about her own.

A wave of revulsion went through her. She didn't want to do anything with her own. She wanted to bury them so deeply she'd never think of them again.

Please, Lord. She passed the oval-framed mirror, a pale ghost in her white nightshirt, and climbed back into bed. *Please let me forget.*

Trying not to think about what was crunching under her feet, Dinah climbed the stairs of the run-down tenement. Tracey forged ahead of her, seeming to be unaffected by the dirt and the smells.

"Do you think the girl will actually go through with it this time?" Dinah didn't really need an answer, but the distraction of hearing Tracey's voice might keep her from tensing up too much as she approached the interview.

"We live in hope." But nothing about Tracey's expression, as she glanced back, suggested hope. Tracey had her game face on. Maybe that was how she coped with what they were about to do.

91

"You're sure she must have seen something?" She made it a question, although she knew the answer.

"Positive. There's no way she stood where she says she did and didn't see the attacker." Tracey's expression softened slightly. "Poor kid. She's immature for a fifteen-year-old. This is going to make her grow up fast."

"Too fast." She knew only too well that experience. It had been hers.

Tracey stopped in front of a door and rapped. "Here we go. Are you ready?"

She nodded, wishing her stomach didn't tie into knots each time she did this. But if it didn't, that might mean she had hardened herself to the victim's pain, and she never wanted to reach that point.

In comparison to the filthy hallway, the inside of the small apartment was almost painfully clean. A thread bare rug covered the floor in the living room area, with flimsy modern furniture placed carefully on it. A large television sat on a metal stand in the corner, and the end tables bore identical vases of plastic flowers atop white doilies.

The girl's mother ushered them inside, almost wringing her hands in anxiety. Tracey had prepped the woman, so she knew to leave them alone with her daughter.

Dinah scanned the living area. "The

kitchen table will be best," she murmured to Tracey, who nodded. Tracey understood that putting a physical barrier like a table between Dinah and the victim would help to make the girl feel safe.

Talking reassuringly, Tracey walked the mother toward what must be a bedroom, while the girl came reluctantly toward Dinah.

So young — that was all Dinah could think. With her parochial school uniform, thick dark braids and slight, undeveloped figure, she looked like a child.

"It's nice to see you, Teresa." Dinah slid onto one of the kitchen chairs, gesturing toward the seat across from her. "I'm Dinah."

Thin lips set in a straight line, dark eyes avoiding contact, the girl nodded and sat down, folding her arms. Behind the girl, Tracey moved quietly to a chair in the far corner of the room, out of Teresa's line of sight.

It wasn't going to be easy. Everything about Teresa screamed that she wasn't going to cooperate. Tracey knew that as well as she did. Still, they had to try.

She looked around for something to serve as a conversation starter. Three framed school photos hung on the wall behind

Teresa — a different Teresa, smiling and eager, a smaller sister with a gap-toothed smile, an older brother, doing his best to look serious in his school blazer and tie.

"I see your mother has your latest school pictures up. My mom always did that, too."

Teresa's shoulders moved in a shrug that could mean anything.

"What are your brother's and sister's names?"

"Margaret. And Joseph." Her mouth clamped shut again.

Clearly small talk was out. Dinah fingered the drawing pad and pencil on her lap, out of Teresa's sight. She might not have a chance to use it.

"Teresa, I'd like to go back to the morning of that day. Will you do that for me?"

A nod.

"Okay, let's start with breakfast. Do you remember what you had to eat?"

They'd have to do this slowly. Taking the witness through the day, letting her recall nonfrightening events, sometimes helped to put her at ease.

Keeping her voice soft and her questions unobtrusive, she led Teresa through the events of the day — breakfast with her family, walking to school with her little sister, classes, lunch.

She didn't look at Tracey, knowing she could count on Tracey not to interrupt. Tracey understood the process, unlike many officers. Teresa had to be led gently to remember, not to guess at eye color or nose shape. This couldn't be rushed, and the wrong question could send them back to square one, perhaps contaminating the memory beyond any hope of accuracy.

Teresa closed her eyes occasionally to visualize what the teacher wrote on the board, what she'd taken from the lunch counter. She glanced to the left, signaling that she was using the remembering part of her brain.

Good. Dinah was there with her, taking a scoop of macaroni and cheese, looking around the lunchroom for a friend. Sitting down with Jessica, who only had hours left to live.

Through supper, the movie, what they talked about as they came out of the theater. Teresa was tensing now, and it was hard not to tense with her. Trauma engraved the scene on the victim's mind, but it also made accessing it wrenching and painful.

"You turned into the alley," she said gently. "Tell me what you saw."

"Dark." Teresa's neck muscles worked, her breathing growing heavy. She crossed her arms, protecting herself. "It was dark. I couldn't see."

She felt, rather than saw, the sharpening of Tracey's attention. The alley hadn't been dark. If it had, the girls probably wouldn't have turned into it. But a streetlight over-hung it, making it look safe.

"Teresa —"

"No!" She shot out of the chair so abruptly that it toppled over. "I didn't see anything! I didn't!" Bursting into tears, she ran from the room. The bedroom door slammed, shuddering from the impact.

"Well." Tracey's eyebrows lifted. "I guess there's nothing on your pad."

Dinah mutely showed her the blank sheet.

"So we got nothing. It happens." Tracey rose.

"We got something." Dinah got up, reaching for her bag, feeling as if she needed something to hang on to. "She may never tell us, and you can't take it to court, but she knows who killed her friend."

Tracey's brows lifted a little higher. "You're sure of that?"

Dinah didn't question how she knew. Some combination of instinct, experience and guidance, probably. But she knew.

"I'm sure. But we may never get it out of her. She doesn't want to remember."

96

She knew what that felt like, only too well.

"Sorry I couldn't get any closer." Marc strolled beside Dinah from the parking space he'd found a block from Marion Square. They were about to tackle the first item on Court's lengthy list of Charleston Christmas events, the lighting of the city Christmas tree.

The cool evening breeze lifted Dinah's dark curls, and she tucked her hands into the pockets of her wool jacket. "This is fine. Do I look as if I can't walk a block?"

Court was several yards ahead. Either he found their pace too slow, or he wanted to give the impression he was alone. It was tough to tell with a teenager. At least he could speak freely to Dinah.

"You look as if you're exhausted. Haven't you been sleeping?"

"I'm fine." She dodged a stroller, shooting him an annoyed look. "Please don't hover. I get enough of that from Aunt Kate."

He shrugged, unconvinced. "If you say so."

The crowds grew thicker as they approached. Families, teenagers and elderly people poured into the area, roped off for the occasion. He remembered Marion Square Park as a bit shabby and run-down, but the city had clearly made an effort to improve things.

He couldn't begin a serious conversation with Dinah in the middle of a holiday crowd, but sooner or later they had to talk. The way she'd looked those moments on the stairs with her white, strained expression still haunted him.

He had to find a way to reassure her that he wasn't going to press her about what happened. Sure, he hoped she might remember something useful, but not at the cost of her well-being. And she'd already given him a possibility, with her revelation of Annabel's attitude toward Carr, the gardener. He hadn't found Carr yet, but he would. He might need to use the firm of private investigators he'd taken the trouble of looking up.

Court slowed his pace and let them catch up with him as they approached the immense Christmas tree at the center of the square. "Have they always done this, Dad?"

"I don't know about always, but I remember going to a tree-lighting when I was a kid. I'm not sure it was in this park, though."

"There are tree-lightings all over the area." Dinah smiled at Court, some of the tiredness easing from her face. "And it's not just to draw tourists, really. Folks like to celebrate, and we're proud of our city, aren't we, Marc?"

He nodded, because to do anything else would provoke an argument. *I'm not part of the city any longer, Dinah. You must realize that. People don't want me here, and I don't belong anymore.*

That shouldn't give him such a lonely feeling, but it did.

"There's Phillips." Dinah raised her hand to wave across the crowd. "He's working one of the charity stands tonight. We should go over and say hello."

He slid his hand into the crook of her arm, anchoring her to the spot. "Later. Looks as if the program is about to start." And he didn't need his son exposed to any more snubs.

He watched Court's face as the tree-lighting ceremony progressed. They'd been to plenty of tree-lighting events over the years, so why did this one impress him so much?

Court stared, rapt with attention, as the Magnolia Singers performed folk carols, and clapped along with the Charleston Community Band. And when the mayor flipped the switch and the sixty-foot tree lit with lights, Court's eyes were as big as they'd been at four or five.

He suspected he knew the answer. This was Court's heritage, just as it had been Annabel's and his. That was what made the difference. In keeping Court away from the possibility of pain, he'd also kept him away from his roots.

When they'd sung the last carol, Court turned to him. "Wow, that was great. How about some hot chocolate? Watching made me thirsty."

Dinah laughed. "I can see how it would." She linked her arm with his. "There's a stand across the way — let's go."

So apparently he was going to see Phil tonight whether he wanted to or not. Dinah didn't even question that — of course they'd go to the stand where Phillips was working. He'd opened this up when he'd insisted on going to the Alpha Club tree sale, so they both knew Phillips was still a friend, in spite of his wife's attitude.

When he saw them approaching, Phil's face broke into the singularly sweet smile he remembered from when they were boys together.

"Hey, it's good to see you." He swung around to fill foam cups with coffee from an urn. "Let me just take care of these customers, and then we can visit."

The moment that took gave him a chance

to study his old friend for the second time. In the glare of the unshaded lightbulb that hung from the top of the booth, Phil's face had lines that aged him, and his hair was more gray than fair.

Still, he, Marc, probably looked older, too. Bitterness had a way of showing on the face.

Otherwise, with his lean, ascetic face and thick glasses, Phil looked like what he was — a historian more comfortable in Charleston's past than the present.

"There now." No one waited for service but them. "What can I get you? It's all for charity, remember, so don't be stingy."

"Hot chocolate all around," he said. Margo was nowhere in sight, and Phil obviously felt free to be friendly without her intimidating presence.

Phillips poured the chocolate and handed the cups across the counter. Dinah wrapped her fingers around the cup as if seeking its warmth.

"I'm glad I had a chance to see you again." Phil's eyes fixed anxiously on his face. "I wanted to say I'm — I'm sorry about what happened the other night. Margo gets these ideas in her head, and nothing can get them out."

She thinks I'm a murderer. Nothing to be gained by repeating the obvious. "It's not your responsibility, Phil. I just hope Margo doesn't speak for you."

"No, of course not." Phil flushed slightly. "I know you didn't hurt Annabel. The very idea is ridiculous."

"James doesn't think so." That still stung. He and James and Phil had been like brothers when they were cadets at the Citadel. He'd thought then that nothing could ever come between them. They were going to save their beautiful city together — Phil as historian, James as politician, he as crusading prosecutor.

"I know." Phil's gaze dropped, as if he didn't want to admit how deep the breach went. "James has changed since, well, since you left Charleston. I thought once we'd be friends for life, but now we don't seem to have a thing in common. I wish life didn't —"

Before he could finish the thought, a bevy of teenage girls came giggling and nudging each other to the counter.

"Sorry, I'll have to take this." Phil checked his watch. "My helper should be here by now. He's late."

"Would you like me to help, sir?" Court set his cup down on the counter. "Just till he gets here?" Court glanced at him. "It's okay, isn't it, Dad?"

He suspected the presence of several cute girls had something to do with his son's sudden altruism. "Dinah may want to get home."

"I'd like to stay," she said quickly. "Let's find a bench and watch Charleston go by until Court's ready. Court, we'll be right nearby, so come and find us."

He nodded, and while Court hurried into the booth, he and Dinah walked down the path to the nearest bench.

It was surprisingly private, screened by azalea bushes, even though it was just a few feet away from the booths. Dinah sat down with a little sigh and sipped at the chocolate.

"You look wiped out," he said bluntly. "Don't tell me to mind my own business, Dinah. Is our being here upsetting you that much?"

She looked at him, eyes wide and startled. "It's not you and Court. It's the case." She shrugged, lips curving in a rueful smile. "Was I rude earlier? I'm sorry. Aunt Kate fusses over me so, and Alice — you remember Alice Jones, her housekeeper?"

"Round, comfortable, the best pies I ever ate. She's still there?"

She nodded. "A little rounder, probably. She keeps offering me chamomile tea. Says it's good for the nerves."

103

He propped his arm along the back of the bench, leaning toward her. "Okay. I promise not to offer you any chamomile tea. Can you tell me about the case, or is that a breach of protocol?"

"Probably, but there's not much to tell. She broke the interview off today before we could get what we need." Dinah seemed to be looking back, probably weighing whether she'd handled the girl right. "I guess I'm disappointed not to come away with a lead."

"It's more than that, isn't it?" He touched her shoulder lightly. "You identify with this girl. Her experience is too similar to yours."

Dinah stared out across the park, as if mesmerized by the thousands of twinkling white lights draped from the trees. "I feel empathy for her, I suppose. But there's one big difference. We're sure she must have seen something, if she can just let herself remember it. I didn't see anything."

He knew better than to question that. It was what Dinah believed, and arguing wouldn't change that.

"Still, a case like this, with a young girl, must be especially painful."

She nodded, still not looking at him. Talk to me, Dinah. Please, talk to me.

She tilted her head back, dark hair flowing across the collar of her cream wool jacket. "I guess that's part of it. Her mother doesn't know what to do to help her, any more than Aunt Kate knew."

"Your aunt sent you away."

"To her cousins in New Orleans. Bless their hearts, they didn't know what to do with me, either." She smiled faintly at the memory.

"Still, you got through it somehow." She should have had more help. Professional help. He should have insisted, though he'd had no right or say.

"Going to art school was the best thing that could have happened to me. In a way, I painted out all my grief and anger. I think I started to find my way once I'd done that."

Have you found your way, Dinah? Or are you still hurting?

He didn't dare to ask the question, but he probably already knew the answer. She was hurting, and his presence made that pain worse. He couldn't even comfort himself with the idea that it would be best for her to face the past, because that wasn't his motive. He was using her, and that was an ugly thing to find in himself.

"Dinah —" He wasn't sure how to put his feelings into words. "Court and I can't leave here with so many questions unanswered. But maybe you should back away." He shook his head. "That wasn't what I wanted to say to you, but you're forcing me to be honest. And maybe what's honestly best for you is to stay away from us."

She turned toward him, her cheek brushing his fingers with a touch soft as a snowflake. She gave him a grave, sweet look. "A few days ago I might have agreed. But now — it's too late for that, Marc. I'm in this thing with you and Court. All the way."

His throat tightened. "Thanks, sugar." The Southern endearment came to his lips without thought. "I'm glad you're on our side."

He'd gotten what he wanted. He should be happy. But all he could think was that now he was responsible for Dinah, too. If this situation hurt her, which it very well might, then he was to blame.

Six

Dinah perched on a stool at the kitchen counter, watching as Glory rolled out crust for chicken pot pie. She might have been a teenager again, escaping to the kitchen for a quick chat with Glory.

Escaping? She took a closer look at the word her subconscious mind had chosen. She'd loved staying in the house with Annabel and Marc that summer, helping to care for Court. Why on earth would she have wanted to escape that?

She hadn't. That was all. Her mind had made a silly misstep. She picked up a scrap of dough and rolled it idly through her fingers.

"So." Glory's black eyes were bright with curiosity. "What you think about Mr. Marcus coming back here like this?"

The soft Gullah cadences of Glory's speech were soothing, even though the question wasn't.

She hesitated. She could trust Glory, but what did she really think about Marc's return, underneath her concern for Aunt Kate and Court and Marc himself?

"I think he had to do it," she said finally. "He had to put things to rest here. I just wish I knew what other things his coming will stir up." James Harwood's animosity flickered through her mind. That had to hurt Marc, as close as they'd been.

"Always a danger of that." Glory's strong brown arms wielded the rolling pin like a weapon. "Folks don't like prodding into the past for a lot of reasons — some good, some not so good."

Dinah had twisted the fragment of dough into a tortured shape. She tossed it into the waste can and dusted her hands. "That's what I'm afraid of, I guess. That he'll stir up something he can't control."

Glory's lips twitched. "Don't know as anybody gonna stop him, though."

"Certainly not me."

Although she probably had as much influence over Marc now as anyone did. Odd. At first, he'd tried to treat her as if she were still that sixteen-year-old, but the more they were together, the more that wore away. Now they talked like friends, for the most part. Except when she tried to get in the way of what he wanted.

No, no one would stop Marc.

The kitchen door swung, and he came in. Glory sent him a smiling glance. "Ain't no use you coming in here now, looking hungry. Supper won't be ready for an hour, and I cook faster without a lot of people cluttering up my kitchen."

"Dinah's here." He smiled at her and leaned against the counter next to her. "Doesn't she bother you?"

"Dinah knows how to make herself useful." She slid a baking tin toward Dinah. "You go on and make some cinnamon crisps out of that leftover dough. Maybe that'll keep these boys from starving till supper's ready."

Marc's lips twitched at being referred to as one of the boys, as if he were no older than Court.

"What's the matter? Doesn't your housekeeper in Boston order you around?" She obediently began rolling out the dough scraps, trying to get the dough as thin as Glory did.

"We don't have a housekeeper now. Just a cleaning service that comes when we're both out and does its work invisibly."

"Sounds a little impersonal."

"I'm sure that's how they prefer it." He

seemed to be watching Glory slide the pot pie into the oven, but his expression indicated that his thoughts were elsewhere. "You didn't make pot pie that last summer we were here, did you?"

Glory closed the oven door and wiped her hands on her apron. "Pot pie's not a summertime dish, to my way of thinking. Heats up the kitchen too much. You want things that cook faster in the summer."

Clearly Marcus wanted Glory to talk about that summer. So Dinah would steer the conversation in that direction, even though her instincts were to do anything but that. "Or cold dishes. You still make the best potato salad on the Peninsula?"

Glory grinned. "Child, I make the best potato salad on both sides of the Ashley and the Cooper," she said, naming the two rivers that bound old Charleston into itself. "Maybe even in Charleston, Berkeley and Dorchester counties all put together."

"I remember that potato salad," Marc said. "Sometimes we had Sunday lunch out on the veranda — potato salad and cucumber sandwiches and crab salad."

"Stop, you're making my mouth water. And Glory won't make us potato salad. It's not summer."

It wasn't any summer, but especially not

that summer, ten years ago, when they'd lunched on the veranda, laughing at Court's attempts to catch one of the butterflies that hovered over the buddleia bush. There hadn't been any shadows of impending tragedy over those lunches, had there?

Glory straightened, hands on her hips. "No sense you talking about potato salad, Mr. Marc. You want to ask me something, just come right out and ask it. You know I'd do anything at all I could for you."

That was a vote of confidence, and she hoped Marc appreciated it. Glory believed in him.

"Thank you." His voice softened a little. "It's not any one question I want to ask you. It's that I hope you'll think about what it was like here that summer. Think about any little things that happened that didn't feel quite right, even if they don't seem to have to do with my wife's death. We don't know what might be important."

Glory nodded, her eyes shadowed. "Reckon I've spent plenty of time on my knees about it. There's nothing that pops into my head, but I'll think on it some more."

"What about Jasper Carr? Do you remember anything about him?"

Dinah had put Carr into his mind with

her simple comment about Annabel not liking the man. She hadn't meant anything by the words — they'd just popped out, and Marc had seized on them.

His single-mindedness chilled her. If Marc did find evidence that implicated someone in Annabel's death, what would he do? Turn it over to the police, or try to take matters into his own hands? She hadn't thought that far, and she should, before she said anything else that might make him suspect someone.

Glory was shaking her head slowly. "Can't think of anything, except that time I found him in the kitchen. But you already know about that."

"Found him in the kitchen?" His voice was sharp, his prosecutor's voice. "What are you talking about?"

"Why, that one evening I came back for my purse. I'd gone off without it. Everyone was out, and there Carr was right here in the kitchen."

"Doing what?" Marc leaned forward, intent.

She shrugged. "Nothing that I could see. He said the back door was open and he just come in for a drink of water, but I didn't buy that. I spoke to him pretty sharp and sent him off with a flea in his ear, I can tell you that."

"Why did you say I knew about it? I didn't."

"I told Miz Annabel the next day." Distress caught at her voice. "Had to do something, didn't I? She said she'd talk to you about it. Said you'd have to give him his notice. Didn't she tell you?"

"No. No, she didn't tell me." He swung toward her. "Did Annabel tell you about it?"

"I don't think so. Not that I remember, anyway."

Impossible to tell what he was thinking, but something implacable hardened his features, turning him into a stranger.

He zeroed in on Glory again. "When was this? Do you remember?"

"I couldn't forget it." Her voice went low and mournful. "It was just a few days before Miz Annabel died."

"Court, if you eat any more of that raw cookie dough, your stomach is going to explode." Dinah tried to sound severe, but judging by the grin on Court's face, he wasn't intimidated.

"That's an old wives' tale, isn't it?" He put another dollop of sugar-cookie dough in this mouth and spoke indistinctly around it. "There's nothing in them before they're baked that's not there afterward."

He perched on the edge of the solid oak table in the kitchen, no doubt getting flour all over his jeans. Well, that didn't matter. Jeans could be washed, and at least the Christmas cookie baking could keep both of them from brooding about where Marc had gone.

"Maybe not, but that's what Aunt Kate always told me. And since she's the one who taught me to make sugar cookies, the advice comes with the cookies."

"Not your mom?"

So few people ever mentioned her parents anymore that Court's innocent question raised an unexpected pang of grief. Everyone else knew what had happened to them, so she never had to explain.

She forced a smile. "My mother wasn't much of a cook. She was more into outdoor things like riding and sailing." Always alive, so alive, with her dark hair blowing in the wind and her eyes sparkling.

"She and your dad both died, didn't they?" Court's mobile face went somber.

Not the happiest of conversations to distract him, but she couldn't tell him anything but the truth. "I was nine, the year Hurricane Hugo hit Charleston. We had a cottage out on Isle of Palms then. My parents were trying to save it."

Foolish, so foolish. None of those houses had been saved from the fury of that storm. They'd risked their lives for a thing of nails and boards, leaving their daughter alone.

"Where were you?"

"They'd brought me in to stay with Aunt Kate." The image of her mother's face was clearer than her own, reflected in the dark glass of the microwave on the countertop. She'd gone out the door laughing and waving.

We'll be back soon, Dinah, and we'll tell you all about it. Be a good girl.

But they hadn't come back. Others had come to tell the story of the cottage collapsing. But she had done her best to be a good girl, hadn't she?

She shook her head. She'd intended to keep his mind off his father, not plunge him into another sad tale. "Okay, let's get back to these cookies. How are you at decorating?"

"Don't know. I never tried. What do I do?" Court bounced off the table, the tea towel he'd tied around his waist flapping.

"You can be as creative as you want with these." She plunged a small spatula into a bowl of icing and coated the surface of a Christmas-tree-shaped cookie. "There's icing in tubes and sprinkles in different colors, too. Have a ball with it. Just remember people might actually want to eat them."

"Gotcha." He wielded a spatula enthusiastically. "Dad doesn't have much of a sweet tooth, but I'll bet he'll eat a couple when he gets home." Court glanced at the clock. "You think he's going to be much longer?"

"I don't know."

She hoped not. Of course it was inevitable that he'd go looking for Jasper Carr, after what Glory had revealed the day before. And it was probably equally inevitable that he'd brush off her suggestions to discuss it with the police or turn it over to the private investigator he'd talked of hiring.

She couldn't protect Marc from himself, and she didn't seem to be doing a very good job of protecting Court from worrying about him.

"I'm sure he's fine. He said he'd be back for supper, didn't he?"

Court nodded, apparently intent on the cookie he was decorating. "He should have let me go with him. I'm not a little kid."

What could she possibly say to that? Fortunately she didn't have to reply, as the front doorbell began to peal.

"I'll get it." She pulled off the oversize apron that belonged to Glory.

"It can't be Dad. He has his keys with him."

She pushed through the swinging door into the hallway. Funny, that was probably the first time she'd heard the doorbell since Marc had come back. Charleston hadn't been beating down his door coming to call.

The frosted glass panel on the front door distorted the figure beyond. She swung the door open, her eyebrows lifting in a polite question when she saw that the man was a stranger. "May I help you?"

"Devlin. Mr. Devlin. I want to see him." He clipped the words off, and one hand beat a tattoo against his leg.

She didn't know him. Did she? Tall, painfully thin, with sunken cheeks and sparse gray hair. Nothing rang a bell, but still something about him seemed faintly familiar, like an old photograph she couldn't quite recognize.

"I'm sorry, but he's not here right now. May I give him a message for you?"

"No. No message. I'll wait." He took a sudden step toward her, and it was all she could do not to retreat.

"I'm sorry. You'll have to come again another time." She swung the door toward him, feeling her pulse quicken. This wasn't right. The intensity that came flooding from

117

the man wasn't normal.

He swung one arm up, blocking the door and sending shock waves through her. "I have to see him." He shoved. Her feet slid on the polished floor as her pulse notched upward. He was going to come in. She couldn't stop him —

"No!"

Court's voice was so like Marc's that for an instant she thought he was there. Then his strong young hands grabbed the door and shoved. The door slammed shut. She snatched the dead bolt and twisted it. Safe. They were safe.

Thunderous blows hit the door, making the glass tremble. She winced away.

"Come on." She grabbed Court's hand. "We've got to call the police."

They ran together back to the kitchen, where she grabbed the cell phone she'd left on the counter, punching in 911.

"An intruder is trying to break into the house." She could only hope she sounded calmer than she felt as she gave the address.

"Officers are on their way." The dispatcher's voice crackled in her ear. "Don't hang up. Keep talking to me."

"He's coming around the house." Court hung on the sink to look out the side

118

window. "He's going to try getting in the back."

"He's coming to the back of the house." She relayed the words, heart thudding. Court — she had to keep Court safe. *Please, Lord, show me how to keep Court safe.*

"Go to an inside room and lock the door." The dispatcher's voice was sharp. "Don't come out until you know the officers are there."

She swung around. "Someplace with a lock." Maybe Court's mind was working better than hers was. Not the pantry — it didn't lock. Her mind cringed at the idea of being trapped in the cellar.

"Powder room," Court said. He seized her hand and grabbed the wooden rolling pin from the table. "It locks from the inside."

She had a quick image of the man's face, framed in the back window, as they raced back through the swinging door, into the tiny powder room under the stairwell. Slam the door, lock it, switch on the light.

Court's face, in the glow of the overhead light, was excited. Not afraid. Excited.

"Wow, Dinah. Nothing like this ever happens at home."

"Trust me, it doesn't usually happen here." She was still clutching his hand, and she wasn't about to let go. "That's generally considered to be a good thing." She pressed the phone to her ear. "We're locked in the powder room. I can hear him banging on the back door. If he gets in —"

"The patrol car is nearly there. Just hang on a few more minutes."

She nodded, then realized how ridiculous that was. The woman couldn't see her.

But Someone Else could. Heedless of how Court would react, she put her arm around him and closed her eyes.

"Dear Father, put Your protection around us now. Keep us safe from harm." Another volley of crashes against the back door came, and she winced. *"We trust in You, Lord. Amen."*

"Amen," Court echoed softly.

Please, Lord —

The wail of a siren punctuated the prayer. The police were here.

Marc screeched to a halt in front of the house, heart pounding, mind whirling with fear and jumbled prayers. *Let them be all right. Please, let them be all right.*

Neighbors clustered on the walk, defying the genteel traditions of Tradd Street by craning their necks to watch the police load a man into the back of a black-and-white. Leonard Hassert.

Marc's stomach clenched as he recognized the man and remembered his angry, shouted threats at the prosecutor when the jury convicted him.

He ran up the walk, brushing past the uniformed officer on the veranda and raced inside. "Court! Dinah!"

Court exploded out of the family room and into his arms. He held his son tightly, heart twisting in his chest. He couldn't lose Court, no matter what, he couldn't. *Thank You, Lord.*

"Where's Dinah? Is she all right?"

"I'm fine." Dinah stood in the doorway of the family room. She managed a smile, but fear still haunted her eyes. "We're both fine. If I ever have to be locked in a powder room with someone while a maniac pounds on the back door, I'll take Court."

Court freed himself, flushing a little. "Hey, you were pretty tough yourself."

"I wasn't the one who thought of the rolling pin as a weapon. I'm just glad we didn't have to use it."

"He didn't get into the house?" His mind started working again, now that the primal need to protect them had eased.

"No, thanks to the new lock you put on the back door."

"The police got here in time." Court

grinned. "Boy, was I ever glad to hear that siren."

"Not as glad as I was," Dinah said, smiling at him. "You thought the whole thing was thrilling — admit it."

Dinah and Court had moved to an entirely new plane in their relationship. That was what facing danger together did for them, apparently.

But they shouldn't have had to. It was no thanks to him that they were safe. God had answered his prayer, but left him with a load of guilt. He hadn't protected them.

"Do you know who that guy was, Dad? The police want to talk to you about him."

He owed Court an honest answer. But not, perhaps, too many details.

"His name is Leonard Hassert. I sent him to prison, back when I was a prosecutor."

Hassert. The name echoed in his mind. Hassert had threatened him. Hassert had been out of jail, pending appeal, when Annabel died.

"Did he —"

Dinah stopped Court's eager questions with a hand on his arm. "The detectives are waiting to talk to your dad, remember?"

"Oh, right." Court jerked a nod toward the family room. "They're in there. Come on."

Dinah's fingers tightened. "I think they want to see him alone. Let's go clean up that mess we left in the kitchen, okay?"

She looked back, her eyes meeting his, as she and Court started down the hallway. Funny. He almost felt that she was telegraphing him a warning.

No warning was needed. For the first time in years he was looking forward to talking with the police. Adrenaline pumped through him as he headed toward the family room. After this, they'd have to admit that Hassert was a suspect in Annabel's death.

He stopped short in the doorway, eyes on the man who rose to meet him. Draydon. Lieutenant Alan Draydon had been in charge of the investigation into Annabel's death ten years ago. He'd made no secret of the fact that he'd thought Marc as guilty as sin, even though he couldn't find enough evidence to take it to trial.

That was then. This was now. Now he wasn't in a state of shock over his wife's death. Now he could make Draydon see that Hassert was a viable suspect.

"Lt. Draydon." He didn't bother to offer his hand. The man wouldn't take it. Ten years hadn't changed Draydon all that much. A few more pounds, a little less hair. He still had a vague resemblance to a bulldog with those drooping jowls and sleepy eyes.

The sleepiness was misleading. Draydon was an aggressive detective — probably a good one, even though he'd been wrong in Marc's case.

"Mr. Devlin." Draydon's lips winced in what might have been intended for a smile. "So you've come back to Charleston. I always thought you would, eventually."

He chose to ignore what was probably meant as a veiled threat. "I'm back. And that seems to have stirred up Leonard Hassert."

"We'll investigate him. Probably take another look at your wife's death." Draydon gestured toward a chair. "Have a seat, Mr. Devlin. I've been looking forward to talking to you since I heard you were back." He smiled, and this time he actually seemed to be getting some enjoyment from the situation. "It's always good to have another chance to close an open case."

Dinah had been right to send him that look of warning. Draydon wasn't focused on Hassert. He had zeroed in on the husband, just as he had ten years ago.

He hadn't succeeded then. Now, Draydon clearly thought he had another chance to prove Marc guilty of Annabel's death.

SEVEN

Dinah crossed the street slowly the next afternoon, aware of subtle changes in the atmosphere of the block. Some of the houses seemed closed to the neighborhood, their drawn shades proclaiming their noninvolvement. At others, lace curtains twitched as her neighbors watched her approach the gate to Marc's garden and push it open.

Well, they'd get over it. Wouldn't they? Surely they couldn't hold a grudge against her forever for her association with the disturbance the day before.

One positive thing had come out of it. Court was even now having tea with Aunt Kate, at her invitation. She wasn't sure Court appreciated the tea, but he seemed engrossed in Aunt Kate's stories of the family. She had it all at her fingertips, back to the first Westlake who'd come from London to the fledging colony in 1697. Her cheeks had been pink with excitement at having a new audience for her tales.

While Court was pleasantly occupied, she had to talk to Marc. There had been no chance the previous day. He'd obviously not wanted to discuss the police reaction in front of his son.

But she'd seen the worry he tried to hide. His conversation with Lieutenant Draydon hadn't gone well. Not that she thought it would. She'd sensed Draydon's animosity only too well.

She walked through the house, expecting to find Marc in the study. It was empty, as was the family room.

She found Glory in the kitchen, slicing onions on the counter. Glory gave her a long, serious look.

"Hear y'all had some excitement here yesterday."

"Too much excitement. Believe me, I could have done without it."

"So could the neighbors, I reckon." Glory jerked her head toward the back door. "Mr. Marc's out there. Some no-count left a message on the garage."

"Oh, no." It didn't seem a strong enough response. "People don't do things like that here."

Glory's knife thudded against the wooden cutting board. "Looks like they do now. He didn't want Court to see it, but there's not much gets past that boy."

"I'd better go and talk to him."

She went out the back, trying not to think about Hassert standing there, pounding on the door. A few steps took her to the garage. She rounded the corner and stopped, stunned. Glory had warned her, but she still hadn't been ready to see the word *Murderer* in foot-high red paint on the back of the garage.

Marc, in jeans and a faded Citadel sweatshirt, was painting over the letters.

It took a moment to find the right casual tone. "It looks as if it will take a couple of coats."

"Afraid so." Marc's even voice didn't give anything away, but his jaw was tense and he didn't look at her.

"Marc, I'm so sorry. It shouldn't have happened." She took a step toward him, not sure how to deal with the anger he had under such iron control.

"Obviously the neighbors didn't care for the police cars on their doorstep. I can hardly blame them."

"Let me help." She bent to pick up the second brush that lay next to the paint can.

He shook his head sharply. "Leave it alone, Dinah. You'll get dirty."

"I don't mind —"

"Leave it, I said." His voice roughened. "Consider this thing a warning for you, too."

She took a breath. "Are you telling me to stay away from you?"

"I should." He put the paintbrush down and swung to face her, planting his hands on his hips. "I put you in danger yesterday just from being in my house." His jaw twitched. "And my son."

"You weren't responsible for that man's actions."

"I should have realized something might happen."

He couldn't seem to let go of his guilt. And there was nothing she could do to help him.

"What did Draydon say? What's happening to Hassert?"

"He's in jail at the moment, but he probably won't stay there for long. They'll plead it out. After all, he didn't actually get into the house."

"And Draydon?"

"You already know what Draydon thinks, don't you? You saw that yesterday."

Yes, she'd seen. "He'll investigate. He's a good cop, Marc."

"Yes. He is." Marc slapped paint on the garage wall. "He won't let his personal belief

128

keep him from investigating thoroughly. But at rock bottom, he believes he knows who killed Annabel. Me."

She didn't know what to say at the pain in his voice. "Marc, maybe you and Court should just go back to Boston."

"I can't. It's too late for that. It's opened up again now. I have to go all the way." He shook his head. "I tried to convince Court to join some friends on a ski trip for the holiday. He won't go."

Of course he wouldn't. "He's just like his father. Stubborn."

His mouth twisted. "I have to keep him safe. And you. I can't let what happened yesterday happen again."

What would it take to make him understand? "You're responsible for Court, but not for me. I make my own decisions. I'm one of the grown-ups now, Marc."

"So was Annabel." He swung toward her again, and her breath caught. His face was ravaged with pain. "Don't you see? If Hassert killed Annabel, it was because of me. So, in a way, Draydon's right. I am responsible for Annabel's death."

Marc hesitated as they came out the red door of the church, wondering if he should offer his arm to Kate Westlake. Or would that be presuming too much? She had invited him and Court to attend services today, but her attitude toward him still verged on the frosty.

Kate, as if she'd measured his thoughts, linked her arm firmly with Dinah's and went carefully down the steps to the sidewalk. Court had been looking at a brochure on the Circular Church's history as he exited the sanctuary, but now he caught up with him.

"Hey, Dad, did you know this church has been here since 1681?"

Dinah, overhearing him, smiled. "Well, not this building. This congregation. This is actually the third building on the site."

"Westlakes have attended services here since the earliest settlers." Kate tapped him on the arm. "That's part of your roots, too, Courtney."

"I'll remember, Aunt Kate." Court gave her the sweet smile that was so like Annabel's.

Her faded blue eyes glistened briefly. "You're very like your mother. You know that, don't you?"

Court nodded, probably a bit embarrassed to bring on so much emotion.

Kate might not have accepted Marc, but she'd accepted his son. Or did she just think of Court as Annabel's son?

The fierce family pride of hers might have something to do with her sudden thawing. Either Court had won her over, or she was announcing to the neighbors that the Westlakes were not to be trifled with or insulted.

Well, either way, he was glad Court had a chance to get to know her. Kate was a piece of family history herself, the classic repository of all the family stories and legends. It would have been wrong to prevent Court from appreciating that.

To his surprise, Kate had actually talked to Court about Annabel. Court had come home from their little tea party clutching photographs she'd given him of his mother as a young girl. He'd had to struggle to hide his feelings. It probably wasn't cool, at thirteen, to be moved by having some mementos of your mother.

They walked down Meeting Street, thronged with Sunday morning churchgoers, toward the car, Court now holding Aunt Kate's arm, Dinah beside him. Would Kate talk to him about Annabel, if he asked her? About that last summer? She'd made her attitude toward him so clear that he hadn't even thought of it, but maybe since Court had bridged the gap, she'd be more open. It was worth a try.

"You're supposed to talk to the lady you're escorting," Dinah said primly. "Or have you forgotten all you learned about Charleston etiquette?"

"I still remember those Saturday afternoon dance classes, if that's what you mean." The boys pretending to choke at wearing white shirts and ties, the girls preening in their dresses and white gloves. "Court doesn't know how lucky he is to have escaped those."

She looked up at him, smooth brow furrowing. "Has something else happened? You looked worried."

"No, not at all. Well, not any more than I was." How could he be? He wouldn't tell Dinah that he wanted to talk to Kate about that summer. He had no doubt that she'd disapprove strenuously.

They reached the car, and Kate turned toward him. "We always have just a cold lunch after Sunday services. You and Courtney are very welcome to join us, if you'd like."

Kate was thawing, actually speaking to him directly.

"Why don't you allow us to take you two ladies out to lunch instead? I have reservations at Magnolia's, and I'm sure they'll be able to squeeze two more chairs at the table."

He deliberately mentioned the restaurant. Magnolia's was one of the places to see and be seen in Charleston. Kate would really be making a statement if she were willing to go there with him.

Her hesitation was infinitesimal. Then her chin went up. "That sounds delightful. Dinah and I would enjoy accompanying you."

He drove sedately over to East Bay. Kate, who seemed to have appointed herself tour guide, contributed tidbits of history about the buildings they passed. If Court was losing interest, he managed to hide that fact.

Well, he had Kate's company, but getting her alone to have a serious conversation would be considerably more difficult. Between her dragon of a housekeeper and Dinah, they kept her well protected.

He was lucky enough to find a parking space near the entrance. As they approached the door, they found a caroling group in Victorian dress singing to a small crowd that had gathered on the sidewalk. Court stopped, curious as always. Marc nudged Dinah.

"Why don't you and Court enjoy the music for a few minutes? I'll take your aunt in and get her settled. I'm sure she doesn't want to stand." Before any of the three of them could raise an objection, he took Kate's arm and hustled her inside.

The hostess swept them to a white-covered table by the window in one of the elegant dining rooms, with Kate nodding regally and exchanging greetings with at least half the people they passed. Charleston was a small town at its heart, when one disregarded the tourists and the students. Everyone in Charleston society knew everyone else. They'd attended those Saturday afternoon dance classes, gone to the same schools, woven a tight, virtually invisible bond.

He seated Kate, helping her to arrange her formidable fur stole over the back of her chair. "Comfortable?"

"Fine." Her gaze met his. "I assume by all this manipulation that you wish to talk with me."

"I —"

"That's fine, because I wish to speak with you. Does that surprise you?"

He nodded in wary agreement. Never underestimate the power of little old ladies, especially one like Kate Westlake, with generations of Charleston tradition behind her.

"I know that my return has raised talk. I'm sorry if that's distressed you."

A flicker of humor showed in her face. "That wouldn't stop you, however." She waved away any answer he might make. "There's no point in regretting. You're here, and we have to face that."

The waitress interrupted with menus. She announced that the brunch specialty was shrimp and sausage with tasso gravy over grits, and disappeared again to bring the extra place settings he requested.

"Did you have something specific in mind?" He lowered his voice, speaking under the noisy conversation of the tourists at the next table.

"Just this. The sooner this situation is resolved, the better. For Dinah's sake, as well as the rest of us."

"I don't want to hurt Dinah."

"You might not be able to help it. The truth comes at a cost." She shook her head, her fingers trembling a little as she toyed with her spoon. "You wanted to ask me something. What is it?"

She was giving him a chance he hadn't expected. "Yes, I do. Was there anything you noticed that summer, or anything that Annabel told you, that seemed unusual? Anything, no matter how small. A quarrel with

135

someone, someone hanging around the house, anything."

She shook her head slowly, not looking at him. "Nothing that comes to mind. It seemed like any other summer, except that Dinah was staying with Annabel. She'd run in every day, of course, always full of stories about Court."

Dinah, not Annabel. "Annabel didn't talk to you about anything that was going on?" He felt a sense of futility. If Hassert had been the killer, there might not have been anything to notice.

"No." Her voice lowered to hardly more than a whisper, and it was as if she were talking to herself. "I failed her. I didn't mean to, but I failed her."

His attention sharpened. "What do you mean? How did you fail Annabel?"

"Annabel?" She looked up, eyes wide and startled, and he had the sense that for a moment she'd forgotten he was there. "No, I didn't mean —" She pressed a handkerchief to her lips. "Not Annabel. Dinah. I shouldn't have sent Dinah away."

"You said Annabel." He leaned toward her. "Kate, what did you mean?"

She put the handkerchief down and looked around. "What's taking them so long?" Her tone was querulous. "We should be ordering."

He sat back in his chair. He couldn't badger an elderly lady in public. Or in private, for that matter. If he drove Kate to the verge of tears, Dinah would have his head.

He'd have to let it go for the moment. But while they debated the relative merits of tomato bisque with fresh crabmeat or lobster salad, he mulled over her words in the back of his mind.

She hadn't made a mistake or confused the two girls. For those few moments she'd been back in that summer, grieving over some way she felt she'd failed Annabel. She knew something about that time that she wasn't ready to say, and he'd dearly love to know what it was.

Dinah tried to relax as she walked with Marc across the campus of The Citadel that evening, Court a few steps ahead of them in his excitement. She wasn't sure spending the evening at the Christmas concert was such a good idea, with suspicion circling around them like no-see-ums on a summer night.

Still, what else could they be doing that would be more helpful? Once Court had gotten his father reminiscing about his undergraduate days at The Citadel, their attendance was a forgone conclusion.

Court had what Aunt Kate would call a whim of iron. Annabel had been like that, too. Once she'd decided she wanted something, there was never any talking her out of it.

"That's where the cadets stage the Retreat ceremony every Friday during the school year." Marc waved toward the expanse of lawn between the buildings.

"Can we come?" Court asked, predictably.

She could easily read Marc's expression, even in the growing dusk. He didn't really want to relive old school days, not under the present circumstances.

She could spare him that, at least. "I'll call and see if it's on for Friday," she said. "I'm not sure when the holiday break starts. If they're doing it, you and I can come." The long gray lines, marching in precision, the flags fluttering and bagpipes keening — of course Court wanted to see it. Any boy would.

"That'd be great, Dinah." He linked his arm with hers, and the unexpected gesture of affection touched her heart.

Marc's frown grew deeper as they approached the white pavement of the court-yard, The Citadel's battlements rising like a fortress around them. White Christmas lights sparkled from the buildings, and the courtyard was thronged with Charlestonians dressed in their best and cadets in uniform. It pleased her to see females among the cadets. Not many, it was true, but once that had seemed impossible.

She moved a little closer to Marc. Did he have the same wary, on-guard sense that she did? Coming here was entering into the heart of Marc's past, where he was likely to run into any number of people he knew, and have just that many occasions to be snubbed by them.

Marc was well armored, probably, but Court wasn't. She didn't want Court's bright, cheerful self-confidence to be dented by anything that happened here.

The chapel was filling up quickly. Did she just imagine it, or did the buzz of conversation take on a different tone as they went down the center aisle, guided by a cadet in dress uniform?

A lady never shows her feelings in public. Aunt Kate's maxims might seem outdated in today's world, but they were there to fall back on in situations like this. Head high, she slid into the pew next to Court.

They might have been wedged in with a shoehorn. She leaned across Court. "I'm going back to the vestibule to hang my coat

139

up. It'll give us a little more breathing room. Don't give my seat away."

Court grinned. "I'll throw myself across it if anyone tries to sit here."

She worked her way back the center aisle, against traffic, seeing faces where before she'd concentrated on getting down the aisle behind the usher. Phillips and Margo sat in the last pew. Phillips glanced up and gave her a shy smile. Margo looked studiously across the rows of people, as if searching for someone she'd misplaced.

Well, she'd get through life very nicely if she never had to speak to Margo again. But she could feel her cheeks burning as she reached the vestibule.

The coatracks were jammed, of course, but she finally found an empty hanger and stuffed her coat in, heedless of wrinkles. She swung around and found herself staring directly at the Citadel tiepin of the man who stood behind her.

"Why are you cooperating with him?" James Harcourt spoke in a furious undertone, his fingers closing around her wrist. "Have you no loyalty to Annabel? She was your cousin."

Anger spurted through her control. Maybe Aunt Kate could live up to her maxims. It looked as if she couldn't.

140

"Annabel was my cousin," she said. "And Marc was your friend."

"Was. He forfeited that when he hurt Annabel." For the briefest of instants, fierce grief replaced the polished politician's aura that James wore so well. "Annabel would hate you for this."

His intensity, so at odds with the public James, shook her, and for a moment she was almost afraid.

Nonsense. She was letting this situation get to her, and she wouldn't do that.

"James, wake up. That's ridiculous. Annabel would laugh if she heard you say that. Marc didn't hurt her. He couldn't. How are you going to feel when the killer is found and you've already condemned one of your closest friends without even a trial?"

She wrenched her hand free and, not looking to see the effect of her words, she hurried away.

By the time she reached her seat, she was able to smile at Marc and Court in what she hoped was a normal way. It must not have been quite as convincing as she'd hoped, because Marc leaned toward her, a questioning look on his face.

Before he could speak, the organ music swelled, capturing them. She sat back, watching the procession of cadets. She'd enjoy the concert. She would not let the ugliness of suspicion taint what should be a beautiful experience.

Her own intentions probably couldn't have achieved that. But when the young voices rose in the old songs of rejoicing at the Savior's birth, she was so filled with that spirit that there was no room left for anything else.

Perhaps choir directors grew weary of doing the same music year after year, but nothing could have brought Christmas more surely into her heart than this. When a young female cadet stepped forward to sing "Silent Night" with candlelight glowing on her fresh face, tears spilled over. Good tears — the kind that washed away pain and left her feeling free.

The music ended with the final verse of "Silent Night." There were stars in Court's eyes when they stood. "Wow," he murmured.

She smiled. He used that one word to cover a lot of emotion. "It was, wasn't it?" For a moment they smiled at each other, perfectly in accord.

She'd turned to start back up the aisle when it hit her — a wave of uneasiness so strong it made her pause, clutching Court's arm. Someone, somewhere in the crowded chapel, was looking at them with such dislike, even hatred, that it was palpable.

She tried to shake it off. She was imagining things, surely. But she found herself scanning faces as they moved along the aisle. Was it you? Or you?

They stopped at the coatrack while she retrieved her coat. She slipped it on, nodding and smiling as the crowd flowed around them. With a little luck, they'd be out the door without incident.

James stepped into their path. Her throat seemed to close. If he was going to create a scene here, of all places . . .

Marc stood still, hand on his son's shoulder, waiting for James to make the first move.

James nodded finally, the movement as jerky as a marionette. "Marc." Having gotten that far, he seemed unable to get any farther.

She couldn't stand this. With an abrupt movement, she seized his hand. "Merry Christmas, James."

He looked at her, startled, as if he'd forgotten she was there. Then his face twitched in what was probably meant to be a smile.

"Merry Christmas, Dinah." He looked at Marc. "And to you, Marc. And Courtney."

He turned quickly, as if that was all he could manage. "Good night."

"Well." Marc glanced at her. "That was a surprise."

She nodded. "Let's go home."

EIGHT

She was on her way to work, and she absolutely wasn't going to give in to the temptation to check on Marc and Court this morning. Dinah pulled her hair back into the low knot that she considered her "work look" and gave herself a final quick survey in the dresser mirror.

Fine. She looked perfectly normal. A little concealer did wonders to hide the telltale signs of a sleepless night.

No, not entirely sleepless. She'd had the nightmare again, and she'd wakened with her mouth dry and her heart pounding. She'd switched on the bedside lamp and reached for her Bible, seeking solace. It had fallen open to a familiar verse.

For now we see in a mirror dimly, but then face-to-face.

The verse echoed in her mind as she picked up her handbag and the portfolio that contained her drawing supplies. Well, that verse was certainly true enough of the current situation. It was impossible to see clearly what she should do or where the danger lay. The sensation she'd had at the concert, of inimical eyes watching them, sent a fresh shiver down her spine.

Enough. She stared at the silver-framed photograph on her night table, and her mother's face smiled back at her. Lila McKenzie Westlake had never been afraid of anything in her life. What would she think of a daughter who let herself be panicked by an imagined stare?

Imagined, that was the key word. She'd probably just been feeling guilty over having spoken as she had to James.

She went quickly from her room and started down the stairs, running her hand along the polished railing. That outburst had been out of character for her, but maybe it had done some good. At least James had been civil to Marc afterward.

Marc wouldn't let it show, but the defection of people who'd been his closest friends had to hurt so much. In the old days there'd been a photo in his study — Marc, James and Phillips in their gray Citadel uniforms, arms around one another's shoulders, laughing. Their young faces had been like the young faces in the choir. Odd that she

146

remembered that picture so clearly after all this time.

Aunt Kate still sat at the breakfast table when she came down. Dinah bent to give her aunt a quick hug. Aunt Kate had been in an odd mood since the Sunday brunch with Marc. She wasn't sure what was going through her mind.

"I'll bring the newspaper in for you, and then I'm off to work."

"You won't forget to check on the availability of caterers, will you, Dinah?"

"I'll take care of it," she promised, suppressing a sigh. Aunt Kate's sudden decision to hold her Christmas tea this year was going to mean a flurry of decorating and cleaning. Still, if it made her happy, it was a small price to pay.

Getting to know Court had thawed her attitude considerably, and Dinah thought that once she'd talked to Marc, she'd no longer been able to imagine him a killer. But it was the paint on the garage door that had roused Aunt Kate's fury. What was the world coming to, when one of her neighbors could be so uncouth?

So Aunt Kate was throwing down the gauntlet to her friends. Come to my Christmas tea and be polite to my nephew-in-law, or lose my friendship. Once she'd decided to put herself on Marc and Court's side, there was no stopping her.

Dinah went quickly out the walk and then paused in the act of reaching for the newspaper. The magnolia wreath that she and Court had made and hung on the gate was no longer there. Instead it lay in the gutter next to the curb.

The anger that swept through her surprised her with its strength. She'd best not let Aunt Kate know about this. She went quickly out the gate and across the street, seething. Maybe she could get it fixed and up again before Court saw. Really, who would do a thing like that? Her Christmas spirit was taking a beating this year.

The wreath didn't look as bad as she feared when she picked it up. The vandal had simply ripped it from the gate and tossed it, not taking the time to pull it apart. She turned it over. The wire loop they'd put on to hang it from was undone, but she could twist it back into place again.

"Ms. Westlake. Sure is nice to see you again."

The voice startled her. She glanced up to find a man sauntering toward her. A ruddy weather-beaten face, thickly curling reddish hair, a patched denim jacket that strained over a paunch — he looked faintly familiar, but she couldn't place him.

"Good morning." One last twist did it, and she hung the wreath back on the gate. "I'm sorry. I'm afraid I don't remember who . . ." She left the sentence open-ended, hoping he'd rescue her.

"Don't remember me, do you?" He stopped a few feet from her. "I reckon there's no reason you would. But I remember you."

He leaned against the fence, and something in the movement brought a memory back. Annabel, looking out the window at the garden and shaking her head.

That man does more leaning on the fence and talking than he does working. I'll have to speak to Marc about him.

"You're Mr. Carr. You were the gardener for my cousin and her husband."

And Marc had been looking for him unsuccessfully. She sent a glance toward the house. Was Marc home?

"That's right. You were just a kid then. Here you're all grown up now." Both the smile and the way his regard lingered on her were a shade too familiar.

"I know Mr. Devlin would like to speak with you." She put her hand on the gate, pushing it open. "Won't you come in?"

Carr took a step back. "I heard that.

Thought maybe I'd come by. Then I thought maybe I'd like to know what he wants to see me for first."

She couldn't let him get away now that he was here. She made an inviting gesture toward the gate. "He's been talking with people who were here the summer his wife died. I'm sure it won't take long."

"I don't know as I want to get mixed up in that." He shrugged. "Never does a man with a business any good to get mixed up with the police."

"There's no question of the police." At least, not yet. "He'd just like to talk about what you remember."

"Nothin'." He said quickly. "I don't remember nothin' about that night."

Her attention sharpened. Why did he assume she meant the night Annabel died?

"You might remember something that happened that summer that would be helpful."

"I don't." The movement of his eyes gave lie to his words. "But if someone did happen to know something, what do you s'pose it might be worth?"

It was like being handed a live bomb. Carefully. Handle this very carefully.

"If someone knew something about a crime, the best thing he could do would be

150

to talk to the police. If you try to sell information —"

He stepped back farther, eyes widening in an unconvincing expression of innocence. "Hey, I didn't say nothing about selling no information. I don't know anything. Don't you go putting words in my mouth."

She'd gone too far, and she tried to repair the damage. "Just come in and talk to Mr. Devlin, all right?"

"No, ma'am." He spun on his heel. "I don't have nothin' to say." And he went off down the street at something approaching a jog.

She stared after him, frustrated. She'd blown it. She'd have to go and tell Marc that Carr had been here and she'd let him get away. Still, what more could she have done?

She went quickly up the walk and in the door before she could think of some reason to evade the task. She came to a dead halt in the foyer, feeling as if she'd walked into a wall. Or into the past.

The marble-topped stand Annabel had brought from her parents' house stood against the right wall again, opposite the doorways to the front parlor and the family room. The gold-framed mirror that had been a wedding gift hung over it once more, just as it had when Annabel lived here. And the vase on top of the stand held arching sprays of jasmine, Annabel's favorite flower.

Her mind whirled, the aroma touching memories she hadn't looked at in years. Annabel bending over her infant son, black curls falling forward, laughing as Court's baby fingers reached for them. Annabel triumphant and alive in evening dress, as she and Marc got ready for the bar association dinner — sparkling in black and diamonds, Marc, dashing in a tuxedo, eyes only for his beautiful wife.

Dinah took a strangled breath and turned to see Marc standing in the door to the study, watching her. She cleared her throat, fighting for calm.

"I see you've brought some more furniture down." Best if he not see the effect it had on her.

He nodded. "I had a talk with a real estate agent yesterday about putting the house on the market. She looked around and repeated what you said — it will show a lot better if it looks lived-in."

"Did she give you the idea of buying the flowers?" The scent seemed to clog her throat.

"After we brought the stand down, I remembered that Annabel always had flowers there." He touched the jasmine gently. "She liked the way they reflected in the mirror."

"I remember." She wrenched herself away from the past. "I just saw Jasper Carr. He spoke to me, out on the street in front of the house."

"What?" Marc started toward the door. "Why didn't you bring him in? Is he still there?"

"Don't bother. He's left already. I'm sorry. I tried to persuade him to come in and talk with you, but he wouldn't."

He turned back, giving her a quizzical look. "Don't look so tragic about it, Dinah. It's not your fault. It was a slim chance that he'd have anything useful to say, in any event."

"That's just it. I think he might." She hated saying this, knowing it was the one thing that would make Marc determined to find him.

"What do you mean?" He covered the distance between them in a couple of strides, clasping both her hands in his as if she might try to run away. "What did he say? Tell me, Dinah."

"I'm trying." She was. It wasn't Marc's fault that the warm grasp of his hands on hers had robbed her of the ability to think straight, let alone speak. His intensity seemed to be an engine, driving her heart to pound out of her chest.

"Sorry." He loosened his grip but still held her wrists gently in his hands. He'd be able to feel her pulse racing, if he bothered to notice. "I didn't mean to shout. Just tell me what he said. Why did he talk to you?"

Maybe better not to mention what had happened to the wreath. "I was adjusting the wreath on the gate when he walked up and started talking to me."

"I see." He looked as if he saw more than she'd said. But he couldn't know about the wreath.

"He recognized me," she said hurriedly. "I didn't know him right away." She went back over that odd conversation. "He said he'd heard you were looking for him, so I asked him to come in. But then he started being — well, *evasive* is the only word."

"Did he say he knew something about Annabel's death?" It had to cost him to keep his voice that even.

"It was odd. First he said he hadn't noticed anything that summer and there was no point in talking to you. Then he said what if someone had noticed something, would you be willing to pay for information."

"You're sure that's what he said?"

"That was the gist of it." She looked into his face. "That's when I blew it. I said if he knew anything, he had to come forward. He denied saying it, insisted he didn't know anything, and off he went. Marc, I'm sorry. I should have been more tactful."

"Don't beat yourself up over it." His dark eyes were intent, focused on a goal she didn't see. "I'll take it from here."

"But he denies knowing anything."

His lips tightened. "It sounds as if he could be persuaded to remember something if the price were right."

"You can't pay someone for information."

"I'm not the police. I'll do whatever I have to."

She didn't like the way he said that. "You don't know where he is."

"The investigator I hired tracked down some of his favorite haunts. I'll find him." He focused on her. "Look, it won't be much use doing that until fairly late in the evening, and I don't want to leave Court alone here. He wouldn't tolerate the idea of a babysitter, but could you think of something the two of you could do together tonight, just to keep him occupied?"

"Marc, can't you just leave it to that

private investigator? Isn't that why you hired him?"

"No. I can't." The words dropped like rocks.

Nothing she might say would change his mind. Trying would be an exercise in futility.

"All right. I'll think of something to do with Court." Now it was her turn to clasp his hand firmly. "But, Marc, you be careful. Promise me you'll be careful."

She was going to be late at headquarters, but maybe a peace offering would help. She swung by Baker's Café, parked and hurried inside, wishing she had time for one of their signature poached-egg dishes. Instead she ordered an assortment of scones and muffins and surveyed the breakfast crowd while she waited for the order.

Charleston was a small town at heart — she'd always known that. And Baker's Café was popular with the locals, which probably explained why Phillips and James were sitting at a small table a few feet from her, engrossed in conversation. Just a friendly get-together, or were they talking about Marc's return?

She took the few steps that separated them. "James, if you eat Eggs à la Bakers every day, you'll need new suits the next time you run for office."

She'd surprised him into a smile as he looked up from the plate of poached eggs, shrimp and andouille sausage. For a moment he seemed like the old friend she'd known for years, but then his expression frosted over as he remembered their last encounter.

"Dinah." Phillips got up quickly. "How nice to see you. Won't you join us?"

She shook her head. "I'm on my way to work. I just stopped by for some muffins."

James's eyebrows lifted. "Balancing the police department's interests with Marc's must be quite a job."

"On the contrary. We all want justice, don't we?" So James still felt convinced of Marc's guilt, even though her lecture at the concert had seemed to soften him up. A fragment of memory teased her. "By the way, didn't you used to use the same gardener Marc and Annabel did — Jasper Carr?"

"Carr? I remember him. One of a long series of unsatisfactory gardeners we hired. But he left Charleston long ago, for good, I thought."

There was a piece of information she hadn't had. "Do you remember when that was?" Shortly after Annabel's death, perhaps?

He shrugged. "I don't keep track of people like that. Anyway, he's gone."

"Not anymore. I saw him this morning. He spoke to me."

Phillips put down his coffee cup. "Dinah, honey, seems to me the man had an unsavory reputation. You shouldn't be talking to him. Where did you see him?"

That was Phillips, of course, still thinking she was a little girl who had to be protected. Still, maybe it was as well not to give the gossip mill any more fuel. "I just ran into him on the street." She glanced at the counter. "I must go. It's been nice seeing you all."

Politeness dictated she say that, but she wasn't sure "nice" exactly described her feelings as she hurried back to the car. James had given her food for thought, though. It might be worth finding out when Carr had left Charleston, as well as when he'd returned.

"It's frustrating." Tracey slapped a file down on her desk blotter, the sound masked by the usual hum of activity in the office late that afternoon.

Once again they'd had a futile visit with

158

their witness. Teresa would go so far with Dinah but no further. Before Dinah could put a line on paper, she'd dissolve in tears and run from the room.

The case, frustrating though it was, at least distracted her from the disturbing encounter with Jasper Carr, Marc's equally disturbing intentions, and the revelation that Carr had left town sometime after Annabel's death. Maybe, if she put it to her correctly, Tracey could be of help.

"You know what's going to happen, don't you?" Tracey ran her hand through her hair, adding to her wild woman look. "I've got half-a-dozen other cases to work. If we don't get something soon, this will be pushed to the back burner. Somebody will look at it once a year, and that's it."

"I know." Dinah closed her eyes for a moment, picturing the spotless apartment, the work-worn mother, the haunted look in the girl's eyes. "If that happens, she'll never heal. Never."

"That sounds like personal experience talking." Tracey leaned toward her.

She shook her head. "Not really. I've gotten past the trauma."

"Dinah, you wouldn't say that if you could see your face when you talk to Teresa. Every time you look at that girl, it's like you're looking in a mirror."

"No." She pushed that away with both hands. "Anyway, it's not like that. It's just on my mind because I'm concerned for Court."

"Are you sure it's not Marc Devlin you're concerned about?"

"I'm sure." She took a breath. Just ask. "You know, you could do something for me that would help resolve this situation."

Tracey's eyebrows shot upward. "Something I could lose my job for?"

"No, of course not. I just want to locate someone. Jasper Carr. He used to be my cousin's gardener. He apparently left town after her death, but I know he's back, and I'd like to find him."

"That sounds like a bad idea."

"Will you do it?" She knew Tracey well enough to know that she might disapprove, but she wouldn't let her down.

Tracey gave an elaborate sigh. "I suppose. But Dinah, I'm telling you this for your own good. Take a couple steps back from Devlin."

"I can't. I —"

"She's giving you good advice, Ms. Westlake."

She hadn't heard Draydon approach. He stood over them. He'd shed his jacket, his

160

tie was askew, and he looked as if he hadn't slept in a while.

She straightened, feet crossed at the ankles, hands folded in her lap, spine taut — typical Southern lady posture, drilled into her practically from birth. "I don't know what you mean."

"Marc Devlin. Ms. Westlake, you don't want to get drawn in by him." That was surely sympathy in his face.

"Marc did not kill my cousin."

He sighed. "I guess you really want to believe that. But you've been involved in police work long enough to know that the obvious is true more often than not."

"Not this time." She would not let herself respond to the concern on their faces. "Anyway, what about Hassert? He certainly acted like a guilty man."

"Guilty, maybe, but not of this crime," Draydon said. "We checked and double-checked his alibi for the night of the murder before we let him go."

"You let him go?"

He shrugged. "He's out on bail. He's smart enough to stay away from Devlin now, I'd say."

Marc wouldn't be surprised. He'd predicted this outcome, but she hadn't wanted to believe it. "I wish I could be as sure as you are. He didn't look very harmless when he was trying to break into the house."

"Look, Ms. Westlake, I'm only talking to you like this because you're one of us. You're not in any danger from Leonard Hassert." He leaned toward her, his face intent. "It's Marc Devlin you need to watch out for."

Marc pulled his rental car into the garage, trying to shove away the frustration that was eating at him. He'd have to walk into the house and act as if everything was fine. Dinah had been upset enough earlier over her encounter with Jasper Carr. He didn't want to aggravate that by his failure to locate the man, even though he itched to question her again for every single word Carr had spoken.

He walked quickly around the house. Not that he expected to find anything or anyone, but it seemed an instinctive protective measure. The bear, prowling the area around his cave for foes.

Unfortunately, his problems were human, not animal.

Nothing disturbed the serenity of the garden. The white lights Dinah and Court had hung from the low branches of the live oak sparkled like stars in the chill air. The veranda light shone on the magnolia and

162

holly wreath on the door, and the window candles seemed to call a welcome.

Welcome. He hadn't thought about that word in connection with this house in a long time. He put his key in the lock, tapping lightly on the door. No point in alarming Dinah and Court.

But when he walked into the hallway, only Dinah came from the family room to meet him.

"Where's Court?"

Her eyebrows lifted. "Hello to you, too. Court went up to bed a while ago. He said to tell you thanks for asking me, but he doesn't need a babysitter."

"Sorry. Hello, Dinah. I hope he didn't take out his antibabysitter attitude on you."

She smiled, but he thought he detected strain in the fine lines around her eyes.

"Not at all. He was charming company. We went out to Citadel Mall and did some Christmas shopping and then ended up with hot chocolate and pepperoni pizza." She shuddered a little. "His combination, not mine."

"I figured that." He crossed to the family room, shedding his jacket and tossing it on the nearest chair. "That kid has a cast-iron stomach. You wouldn't believe what I've seen him put away for breakfast."

She'd followed him into the family room, and she nodded at the logs glowing in the fireplace. "When we got home he insisted on starting a fire in the fireplace. He wanted to toast some marshmallows, just to top things off, but luckily there weren't any."

"I'm glad for your sake." He sank onto the leather couch, suddenly aware of how tired he was, and patted the seat next to him. "Now sit down and tell me what has you looking so stressed, other than Court's strange tastes in food."

"Nothing." She sat, but her eyes evaded his. "What happened tonight? Did you find him?"

"No." He stretched his legs toward the blaze. He'd have said it wasn't cold enough to start a fire, but it was comforting anyway. "I went to one dreary dive after another in the part of town the chamber of commerce doesn't advertise to tourists. It was the same story everywhere. Carr is a regular, but they haven't seen him in a couple of nights."

"Then he's changing his regular habits." Dinah seized on that immediately. "That must mean something."

"Maybe that he doesn't want to see me." He studied her face. That delicate profile might have been etched on a cameo. "Come on, sugar. I can see something's wrong. You may as well tell me."

"If you go back to Boston and call people 'sugar' they'll have you arrested."

He resisted the urge to smile. "You're stalling."

"It's nothing." She shrugged, focusing on the hands she had clasped in her lap like a schoolgirl. "I shouldn't let it upset me. It's the jasmine."

For a moment it didn't compute. Then he realized she was talking about the flowers on the hall table. "The jasmine? What about it?"

"The scent gave me a headache, for one thing." She rubbed the tips of her fingers between her brows. "But it also made me remember things. Is that why you bought it? Because scents stimulate the memory?"

"I bought it because Annabel used to put jasmine in that vase, that's all." Questions burned on the tip of his tongue, but he had to proceed carefully. "Did the jasmine bring back memories of Annabel?"

What do you remember, Dinah? What memories are buried so deeply you never want to find them?

She nodded slowly, her lips tensing. "It made me think about that summer. Mostly I remember the quarrels. I'd forgotten that." She looked at him then, with what might have been accusation. "You weren't around much, but when you were, it seemed you and Annabel were always arguing."

She was being fair. It was irrational to feel pain at the look in her eyes.

"Yes." He had to take a breath before he could go on. "Sometimes I think that's all I can remember of that time. The arguments. The heat. The pressure at work to succeed."

He stared into the heart of the fire, remembering. There had been pots of flowers in the hearth the day Annabel had thrown a Dresden china shepherdess against the fireplace. Shards of china had sprayed over the flowers.

"What did you fight about?" Dinah's voice had gentled, as if she felt his pain.

"Everything." He shrugged. "Annabel didn't want to be pregnant again, did you know that?"

She shook her head, eyes wide. "But she loved being a mother."

"She did. But we hadn't planned another baby just then. I thought, seeing how she loved Court, that it would be all right. That once the baby came, she'd forget how she'd felt."

"She would have." Dinah's words were quick and warm. "Of course she would have."

He shrugged. "Maybe. But at the time, she hated it. Every symptom was another reason to rail at me. And she hated my job."

"You were such a good prosecutor. I always thought —"

"What?" He put his hand over hers where it lay on the couch between them, wanting to know what that serious-eyed child had thought of them.

"I thought you were a hero, going out to battle the bad guys every day."

"With a writ in one hand and a subpoena in the other." He had to take it lightly, because he'd like to be that hero Dinah imagined.

"I'm sorry you lost that, Marc." She seemed to read right past his words to his heart. "It's not fair."

He shrugged. No point in talking about what couldn't be cured. He'd made a satisfying career for himself, even if it wasn't what he'd dreamed it would be.

"Annabel wanted me to give up prosecutorial work for something more prestigious. I was away too much, I wasn't consorting with the right kind of people — you name it, it became a quarreling point. I'm sorry you heard us."

"I never realized what the quarrel was about. I just knew things weren't right between you. Was that why she wanted me to stay that summer?"

He met her gaze, startled. "I don't know. I never thought of that."

"She may have thought I'd be a distraction. Or a buffer." Her face clouded with sorrow. "I wish I'd been able to give her what she wanted."

He tightened his grip, wanting to reassure her. "That wasn't your job. You were just a kid. It was my job." His throat tightened with the words he didn't want to say. "I hated the quarrels, so I stayed away from the house more than I had to."

"Marc, don't." She turned toward him, violet eyes bright with unshed tears. "You can't blame yourself."

"If I had been here, it wouldn't have happened." He said out loud the words that had festered in his soul for ten years. "I know that, Dinah. I failed her."

"No. No, you didn't." In her eagerness to comfort him, she took his hand between both of hers. It seemed he could feel all that was good and true in Dinah through the pressure of her fingers. "That's survivor guilt. All of us have felt that, but it's not true."

"Not for you. But it is for me."

A tear spilled over onto her cheek and

glistened there. He touched it to wipe it away. Somehow it seemed very important that Dinah not cry over him.

Her skin was warm and smooth against his fingertips, and her eyes shone with caring. For him. All that warmth and caring and honesty that was Dinah drew him toward her until it took all his strength not to pull her against him and cover her soft lips with his.

He couldn't. He shot to his feet and covered the space to the fireplace in a few short strides. The room wasn't big enough. He needed to be farther away from her than this.

The mirror above the fireplace reflected the cozy room — the furniture Annabel had chosen, the Christmas tree that Court and Dinah had trimmed. And Dinah, sitting where he'd left her, a lost look in her eyes.

Feeling anything but a cousinly fondness for Dinah would be a recipe for disaster. A relationship between them in the shadow of Annabel's death would be enough fodder for the gossip mills to last a lifetime. Aunt Kate would die of the shame of it.

Dinah wasn't a child any longer, but she wasn't the tower of strength she'd like to think she was. He'd brought her enough

grief already. He couldn't bring her any
more.

NINE

Aunt Kate's Christmas tea was in full swing, the hum of conversation rivaling a swarm of bees. Dinah pinned a smile to her face and carried a fresh tray of ham-asparagus rolls to the light buffet that had been set out on the dining-room table. She'd almost persuaded Aunt Kate to use a caterer, but Alice had taken great offense at the idea of someone else preparing food to be served in this house.

Several traumatic discussions later, Dinah had accepted defeat. She had finally convinced them to let her bring in some cream puffs and a few savories from a bakery they trusted. Everything else Alice had made, with the help of a niece to do the prep work.

Dinah scanned the table to see if anything else needed replenishing. The cheese bennes were going quickly, of course. No one had the light touch Alice did with the delicate cheese and sesame wafers. She'd been begging Alice for years to let her help make them, but Alice insisted no one else could slice them to the exact thickness of a dime. She'd probably carry her secret recipe to the grave.

She switched the tray for one she had waiting on the sideboard. One good thing about being this busy — she had a reason not to go anywhere near Marc.

He'd barely spoken to her for the past few days. Ever since that night when they'd been so close, to be exact. Her cheeks warmed at the memory of those moments. He'd nearly kissed her, before he'd jumped up and practically run away.

Had he seen something in her eyes that precipitated it? That idea was too humiliating even to consider.

He'd opened up to her, showing her his pain, and she'd responded. That was all. That had to be all. He would never look at her as anything but Annabel's little cousin.

She couldn't think about that now. She had to keep smiling, keep being the perfect hostess. No one must see anything in her face when she looked at Marc.

The pleasant hum of conversation as guests eddied between the parlor and the dining room assured her that everything was going as it should. People had turned out in force this afternoon, a testament to the power the Westlake name still had in Charleston society.

Court, in a navy blazer and gray slacks, hovered next to Aunt Kate's armchair, ready to fetch anything she needed. She was introducing him to everyone, her tone calm and commanding.

"Say hello to my great-grandnephew, Courtney. Annabel's son."

Aunt Kate's words put Court securely in his proper place in Charleston's social strata, and people responded to that. She'd already overhead several invitations to Court to meet this young person or that, participate in one event or another.

As for Marc, well, people were at least being civil to Marc. Etiquette demanded that. She let herself glance at him. He was standing by the bay window, a cup of fruit punch in one hand. Phillips stood next to him, looking as relaxed as she'd seen him lately.

She began to weave her way through the crowd, offering a tray of sweets — tiny cream puffs and éclairs, Alice's rich triple chocolate brownies, pecan tassies. Phillips swerved away from Marc and stopped her, picking up two of the brownies.

"Margo's not here to chastise me, so I'm going to eat what I want."

Dinah raised her brows. "Does she really have a sick headache?"

"Now, sugar, you know better than to ask a man to tell on his wife. Your aunt accepted her excuse."

"My aunt would never let you know if she didn't."

But Dinah had read behind Aunt Kate's smile. Sooner or later, Margo would regret this affront to Westlake family pride. Aunt Kate might no longer take an active role in the complex web of Charleston's social structure, but she still had power. A telephone call, a word dropped in someone's ear, and some committee appointment or invitation that Margo coveted would be inexplicably out of her reach.

"I just wanted to thank you, Dinah." Phillips's gray eyes warmed behind his glasses. "Without you, I probably never would have renewed my friendship with Marc, and I'd have been the poorer for it."

"I'm not sure I had anything to do with it, but I'm glad, for both your sakes. Have you been reminiscing about your Citadel days?"

"We surely have. I tell you the truth, I'd never have gotten through those first weeks without Marc and James. The two of them dragged me bodily through more than one obstacle course. Seems a long time ago, I'm afraid. I couldn't even walk an obstacle course now." He shook his head, smiling. "Maybe I'll get some coffee to go with this brownie."

He headed toward the silver coffee urn on the sideboard, and she smiled after him. It was good to see that relationship mended, if nothing else could be.

"Old friends getting back together, I see."

She turned. James stood behind her, balancing one of Aunt Kate's bone-china cups in his hand. His smooth, polished air was perfectly intact, but there'd been something a little off-key in his words, hadn't there?

"It's nice to see you, James." She hesitated, then spoke impulsively. "Why don't you go and join them? It's not the three musketeers without you."

His cool blue eyes studied her face for a moment before he gave a chilly smile. "What a nice child. You want everyone to shake hands and be friends."

"I'm not a child." Although denying it probably sounded childish. People who had been Annabel's friends would always think of her that way. Including Marc. Something seemed to squeeze her heart. "I just think it's past time for people to move on."

"Can you forget that easily? I can't."

Shaking him was not an option at Aunt Kate's Christmas tea. "I'll never forget Annabel, if that's what you mean." She kept her voice low, although no one seemed close enough to hear. "But Marc is innocent."

"We're none of us as innocent as all that, Dinah." His blue eyes, intent on her face, were like shiny marbles, giving away nothing of his feelings. "Are we?"

"I don't know what you mean." Had she been guilty, with her teenage crush on her cousin's husband?

He shrugged, looking away from her as if losing interest. Or as if disappointed in her. "Some things can't be forgiven, you know. They're too deep a betrayal for that."

"James —"

He thrust the cup and saucer into her hands. "Please make my excuses to your aunt. I'm afraid I'm due at another engagement."

He worked his way through the crowd so quickly he might be escaping, without a single glance in Marc's direction.

Well. She deposited the cup and saucer on a side table. That was odd. Was James talking about himself? Or Marc?

Betrayal. It was an ugly word for an ugly deed. But who had been betrayed, and why?

She found herself moving through the crowd toward Marc without having made a conscious decision to do so. She was a few steps away when he saw her.

His eyes warmed for an instant. Then, very deliberately, his expression changed to something else. Friendly but distant, as if she were a waitress descending on him with her tray of desserts.

"You're not going to offer those to me, are you? Phillips is the one with the sweet tooth."

"And I've had my share," Phillips said quickly. "Dinah, don't you get to sit down and enjoy the party?"

"When it's over." She forced a smile. "Then I'll relax." And then she'd let herself listen to what her heart was telling her.

That she was only kidding herself when she insisted she didn't have feelings for Marc. And that he saw, and knew, and was warning her off.

Whatever impulse had made her decide to brave King Street traffic to get some Christmas shopping done had definitely led her astray. Dinah sat at the light, drumming her fingers on the wheel as pedestrians, laden with far more packages than she'd managed to purchase, made their way across the street.

King Street was dressed in its finest for the holiday season, with lights everywhere and Christmas trees in every window. She should be enjoying this outing, instead of fretting.

Truth was, she'd thought to distract herself from her feelings about the situation with Marc. Unfortunately, she wasn't succeeding.

She should have talked to him about that odd conversation with James Harcourt. But he had made it all but impossible, managing never to be alone with her even when he and Court had stayed to help clean up after the guests had left. She'd thought about going to the house this morning, but turned coward at the thought. So she'd gone shopping instead.

The cell phone interrupted the thoughts that didn't seem to be going anywhere. She checked the number before answering. Tracey. "Hey, Tracey. What's up?"

"Not much." But she sounded harried. "You remember that information you asked me to get for you?"

Her heart beat a little faster. Information on Jasper Carr, the elusive gardener. "Did you find anything?"

A long pause. "Listen, this information isn't going out to any unauthorized person, is it? Because that could bring me grief."

To Marc, in other words. Naturally Tracey would feel that way. "No, it's just for me. I promise."

"Okay, then. He doesn't seem to be at the address that's listed for him, but he's working out at Magnolia Gardens. It's a temp job, just for the Christmas season. You can probably find him there."

"Thanks, Tracey. I appreciate the help."

"What are you up to, girl? Something I should know about?"

"Nothing that has anything to do with the police. I just want to talk to him, that's all."

"Well, you be careful." Her voice was concerned. "Don't do anything stupid."

"I won't."

She hung up, elated. Something, at last, was breaking her way.

Marc would say she should come straight to him with this information. He was the one who needed to talk to Carr. But she'd promised Tracey, and she couldn't go back on that.

So the obvious course was to drive out to Magnolia Gardens and talk to the man herself. She'd been caught by surprise the last time, and she hadn't said the right things to him. This time he would be the one to be surprised, and she'd persuade him, somehow, that he had to talk to Marc.

The light went green. She flicked on her turn signal and made an abrupt right turn, leading to annoyed drivers venting their feelings with their horns. She'd take the expressway over the Ashley River and head up 61.

She had no idea what time gardeners left for the day, but Magnolia Gardens should be open until five. She'd be in time.

Or not. She hadn't thought about how crowded the commercial strip on the west side of the river was this time of day. At least it was moving faster than downtown traffic. Strip malls gradually gave way to housing developments, and the road became what Aunt Kate reminisced that it used to be — oak-lined, moss-draped, low country. The Ashley River gleamed through the trees off to her right now and then.

Once this road had been lined with plantations, their mansions facing the river, until Union troops marched down the road toward Charleston, burning as they went. Now only three were left — Drayton Hall, Middleton Place and Magnolia. They'd all been familiar to her since childhood, but Magnolia was her favorite. Carr had been lucky to find work there.

She took the turning toward the river at the Magnolia Gardens sign. Aunt Kate used to bring her every year to see the camellias at Christmastime, and again in the spring to see the azaleas.

She parked the car. The lot was nearly deserted, probably too late in the day for most visitors. She hurried to the ticket booth. Only one other car pulled in behind her.

"Just an hour till closing, miss," the woman warned as she took the bill she held out.

"That doesn't matter. I just need to locate one of your employees. Jasper Carr. Do you know where he might be working?"

She consulted a clipboard. "Should be down by the Biblical Garden, if he's doing what he's supposed to." She sounded doubtful.

"I'll find him. Thank you." She hurried down the path, buttoning her jacket. The wind was chilly, and she hadn't dressed for this. She could only hope that, for once, Carr would indeed be where he was supposed to be.

The White Bridge over the lake was strung with evergreen swags and wreaths along its railing, and in the distance, she could see the glow of the camellias. She really should try to bring Aunt Kate out while the camellias were blooming.

She went quickly down the path toward the Biblical Garden. It was a favorite spot of Aunt Kate's. She'd been there so often that she no longer needed to walk around and read the signs that described the plants, but simply sat, drinking in the still atmosphere.

Well, Dinah would do no sitting today, at least not if she could help it. Find Jasper, persuade him to cooperate. Maybe she should hint that Marc would be willing to pay for information. Marc had certainly given her the impression that he might.

Hurrying her steps, she rounded the hedge into the Biblical Garden, rehearsing the words she'd say. She stopped abruptly. A long-handled rake leaned against an empty red wheelbarrow. No one was there.

She hadn't realized how much she wanted to find the man. The disappointment was like a blow to the stomach.

Well, his equipment was there, so surely he was around somewhere. "Mr. Carr?" Her voice echoed emptily. No one answered.

She stepped back onto the path outside the Biblical Garden, looking in both directions. Nothing. Still, he hadn't come past her. She'd go on. He wouldn't have left the hoe and wheelbarrow there if he'd quit for the day.

The path led on to the maze. Magnolia's designer had modeled his maze on the one at Hampton Court, but instead of boxwood, it was planted with hundreds of camellias. She walked toward it, captivated as always by the sight.

She stood for a moment, feasting her senses on the delicate blossoms and the dark leaves of the holly bushes that were interspersed with the camellias.

"Mr. Carr?" she called again. No reason to believe he'd gone into the maze. He was probably hiding out somewhere, though, perhaps having an illegal cigarette. "Mr. Carr?" She called again, starting into the maze. The blossoms surrounded her, closing into what had always seemed a magical place.

Christmas camellias, she called them as a child, thinking everyone had camellias blooming for Christmas. She stopped. Was that a step she heard?

"Hello? Is anyone there?"

Again there was no answer, but something brushed against the far side of the bushes on her right.

She froze, apprehension sending chills

snaking down her spine. She opened her mouth to call out and then closed it. If someone was there, he hadn't responded to her previous calls. Instinct told her he wouldn't answer this time.

She ought to feel angry. She didn't. She felt afraid.

No point in standing here, waiting and wondering. She'd go back to the ticket booth, find out where Jasper checked out when he left for the day, and wait for him there.

That was a sensible, practical solution. So why did she feel compelled to creep away like a thief? She took a careful step back from the hedge of camellias, then another. Her breath was soft and shallow as if even breathing might draw too much attention to herself.

I'm being silly, Lord. Or am I? Please, surround me with Your protection.

She reached the entrance to the maze and took a deep breath. It was going to be all right. It was.

She walked quickly along the outside of the maze, breath still coming too quickly. Foolish, to let herself be spooked by being alone here. She wouldn't let her wayward imagination ruin a place she'd always loved.

A few more steps and she'd reached the

corner. She'd just go back —

A blur of movement from the corner of her eye, an arm, a sleeve, someone grasping her, a hand over her mouth. She tried to scream, but the hand was choking off her voice. She struggled, kicking at him, trying to swing her handbag at him. Struggle, fight, don't give in —

"Ms. Westlake, please. Please, don't scream. I won't hurt you."

Please, Lord, please, Lord.

"I won't hurt you, I won't. I just want to talk." He sounded as if he were on the verge of tears, and somehow that seemed to get through the fear.

She twisted around to see his face. Jasper Carr? No. It was the man she'd last seen trying to get into the house. Leonard Hassert.

She pushed away the fear. Fear led to panic, and panic would do no good.

"Please, Ms. Westlake." His voice was trembling, and she realized his hands were trembling, too. "Just don't scream, all right? I'm going to take my hand away."

He moved a step back. She took a breath, the air sweet. Her muscles shook with the effort it took not to run.

"What do you want?" Her voice rasped on the words.

"Not to hurt you," he stammered. "Not that. Please, you have to believe me."

"You picked an odd way to convince me of that." *Give me the right words to handle him, Father.*

"I'm sorry, I'm so sorry. I thought you wouldn't see me if I came to your house, so I followed you."

He was certainly right to be cautious. She'd call the police at the sight of him. He looked so pitiful, standing there with tears in his eyes, that her fear ebbed away.

"All right, I'm here now." She clenched her handbag tightly. "Say what you have to say."

"I have to talk to him — Mr. Devlin. I know he doesn't want to see me. I thought maybe you could talk to him for me. Get him to see me."

She took another step back, and he made no move to stop her. She slipped her hand into her purse, relieved when her fingers closed over her cell phone.

"I'm doing this all wrong." He rubbed his forehead, looking and sounding like a petulant child. "I think about it, but then I don't know what to do."

"Why do you want to talk to Mr. Devlin?" Impossible to go on being afraid of someone who looked so hangdog.

"I wronged him."

"What do you mean?" Her heart jolted. Maybe she'd been too quick to think him harmless. Was he talking about Annabel's death?

"I wronged him," he said again. "I have to tell him. I have to make amends." He reached in his pocket, and she tensed. But his hand came out with a small white card. "He can reach me here. Please, please —"

His voice broke. He turned away, tears spilling over, and lurched into a shambling run down the path and out of sight.

TEN

"I think it would be best if you and Court went over to your house." Marc said the words without any real expectation that Dinah would listen to him.

Sure enough, she shook her head. "I'm staying here." She planted her hand on the hall table, as if to anchor herself. "If Court would like to go keep Aunt Kate company this evening, I'm sure she'd appreciate it."

"No way." Court flushed slightly. "I mean, I like her a lot, but if Dad's going to entertain a murderer, I'm not leaving."

"I doubt very much that Hassert is coming here to confess to murder."

But what was driving the man? His behavior had been odd to the point of dangerous, first trying to force his way into the house and then accosting Dinah that way at Magnolia Gardens. Marc was reminded yet again of her recklessness.

"You shouldn't have gone out there after

Jasper Carr alone. It was too dangerous."

Dinah's chin lifted at the implication that she couldn't take care of herself. "I didn't even find Carr. And I've told you, Tracey gave me that information in confidence. I shouldn't have told you at all, but after what happened with Hassert, I didn't have much choice." She glared at him as if it was his fault.

"You were alone, that's the point. Hassert was obviously following you —" He stopped, because if he thought of how the man had frightened Dinah, he'd be more inclined to punch him than to listen to him.

"If it hadn't been there, it would have been someplace else." She shrugged her shoulders eloquently. "I can't stay inside the house all the time. I won't change my life because of Hassert or anyone else."

"Well, I've agreed to see him. I hope that will end it." He glanced at the grandfather clock. It was nearly eight. "He should arrive soon. I'll hear him out, and then I'll make it clear to him that if he comes near any of us again, he'll be back in jail."

Dinah nodded. "That would do it for any sensible person. Hassert hasn't impressed me as being especially sensible so far."

She'd put her finger on the heart of what bothered him, of the thing that had his

189

stomach churning when he thought of the man being too close to Dinah and Court.

"That's been his pattern, as far as I can tell." He had to speak coolly, rationally, even though what he wanted to do was pick her up and carry her bodily out of the house. "He acts on the impulse of the moment and regrets it afterward. I looked up his case again before we came south. He's not a career criminal."

"Let's hope he doesn't plan to start."

The doorbell rang, and Dinah jerked. In spite of her determined facade, she was nervous.

Without thinking about it, he caught her hand to reassure her. The simple gesture set up a longing to hold her that was anything but simple. He let go as if he'd touched something hot. You're not going to do that, remember?

Dinah looked away from him and grabbed Court's arm. "We'll be in the family room with the door ajar, listening. If we hear anything odd, we're calling the police."

"If I had a baseball bat —" Court began.

Dinah pulled him toward the family room. "No baseball bats. Your father can take care of himself."

Did she really think that? She was afraid, but he wasn't sure whether that fear was for him or Court or herself.

Maybe it didn't matter. The point was it existed, and he'd exposed Dinah to that by coming here and forcing her to choose sides.

He shoved his concerns about Dinah to the back of his mind as he approached the door. He'd have to worry about Dinah later. Right now he needed to focus on dealing with Leonard Hassert.

He yanked the door open with such force that Hassert looked startled. He tried to arrange a less-forbidding expression on his face. If he hoped to get anything out of the man, it would be best not to scare him.

"Hassert. I understand you want to talk with me."

"Yes — yes, sir, I do." He was practically stammering. "May I come inside?"

He took a step back, holding the door open even though his instinct was to slam it in the man's face. "Come in." He nodded to the study door. "In there."

Following Hassert to the study, he watched the way he walked, the way his hands moved, the way he held his head — all the things he would notice in a courtroom when a defendant took the stand. Hassert was afraid, that was certain. He also gave the impression of being embarrassed, hands fidgeting, eyes not meeting his.

Obedient to the promise he'd given Court and Dinah, he left the door ajar. He just hoped they had sense enough not to act prematurely and ruin things.

He nodded to the chair he'd placed in the pool of light from the desk lamp. "Have a seat." The chair behind the desk he'd reserved for himself. It gave him a nice wide expanse of solid mahogany between him and Hassert.

Not that that would help if the man were armed. Well, a person had to take a few chances if he were to accomplish anything.

"You've gone to plenty of trouble to see me." His fingers tightened on a paper knife, and he forced them to relax. "Let's hear what you have to say."

Hassert flushed, the color brightening his pale complexion for a moment, then fading. "I'm sorry. I told Ms. Westlake I was sorry, too. I didn't mean to scare her."

Relaxation wasn't working. "What did you think would happen when you lunged out from behind a bush and grabbed her? Of course she was frightened. She could have you arrested for assault."

Hassert paled again at the threat. Obviously he didn't want to go inside again. "I said I was sorry."

"You acted on impulse, just like you did

when you attacked that man in the bar. You jumped out and grabbed Ms. Westlake without thinking of the consequences."

"I didn't mean anything." He hung his head like a sulky child. "I just had to get you to talk to me. I know I did it all wrong." He looked up, and Marc saw that his pale blue eyes were filled with tears. "I'm sorry. I had to see you. I had to tell you how sorry I am."

He planted his hands, palms down, on the desk surface. "You mean you're sorry for killing my wife."

"No!" Hassert's voice soared, and Marc could only hope Dinah wouldn't be inspired to call the police. "No, I didn't do that. I couldn't do anything like that. You have to believe me!"

"Why?" He kept his voice cold. "Why would I believe you? You told Ms. Westlake you'd wronged me. That's the biggest wrong anyone ever did me."

"You don't understand." Hassert slumped in the chair, and it was hard to believe he'd be brave enough to raise his hand to anyone. "All my life I've had the same trouble. I've given in to anger or fear and done the wrong thing. I always told myself I couldn't help it."

"You threatened me when you were convicted. How do I know you didn't follow through on that threat and come after my wife?"

Panic flared in the man's eyes. Marc tensed. Maybe he'd pushed too hard.

"I didn't do anything to her. I had an alibi. The police checked it."

"Alibis can be faked." He'd thought that all along, but looking at Hassert, his conviction was seeping away. Hassert didn't look or act as if he had that particular sin on his conscience. It had been a long time since he'd practiced criminal law, but the instincts were still there.

"I don't know how to convince you, but I didn't." He shook his head, seeming to shrink in the chair.

"Then why did you say you wronged me? Why were you so eager to see me?"

Hassert's hands twisted together in his lap. What would Dinah say about his body language? She had to be expert at reading that, to do the job she did. Not that he was going to let her get anywhere near Hassert to find out.

"I threatened you. You were doing justice, and I threatened you." Hassert shook his head, seeming on the verge of tears. "When I was in prison, I finally had to face the truth about myself. All the excuses fell away, and the Lord made me see that I was a miserable sinner. But He forgave me." Hassert looked up, smiling through his tears. "I knew I had to try and right the wrongs I'd done. I wasn't able to find you, to tell you that, until you came back to Charleston."

He let out a long breath. Was this for real? It certainly sounded that way. "You went about it the wrong way. You know that, don't you?"

"I know. I'm sorry. I never meant to scare anyone. I just really needed to see you, so I could ask for your forgiveness." He leaned forward, face intent, and gripped the edge of the desk. "Please. I can understand if you don't want to, but please forgive me. I was wrong. I have to ask for your forgiveness."

He didn't want to give it. That was the rock-bottom truth. The man had haunted his dreams for years.

But he'd always trusted his instincts, and they were telling him that Hassert hadn't had anything to do with Annabel's death.

And if someone asked for forgiveness, what else could he do? *Forgive us our trespasses, as we forgive those who trepass against us.* It would be hard to go on praying that if he couldn't forgive.

His throat was so tight he wasn't sure he could speak. He stood, taking his time, studying the man who rose when he did and stood there with pleading on his face.

"I forgive you." He cleared his throat and held up his hand before the man could speak. "But I want your word that you won't approach my family again, and that includes Ms. Westlake. This closes the books between us. Agreed?"

"Agreed." Relief flooding his face, Hassert wrung his hand. "Thank you, sir. Thank you."

Marc nodded. He ought to feel relieved. But as he showed Hassert to the door, he could only think one thing. This meant that Annabel's killer was still out there, somewhere. Watching. Waiting.

"How soon is it going to start?" Court, impatient as he always seemed to be, leaned forward in the back seat, staring out at the Cooper River, serene in the dusk.

"The boats start moving at five o'clock, but it'll take them a while to get downriver this far."

Court had found the Christmas Parade of Boats on the Internet, and he'd been fully prepared for nonstop nagging to get his father to agree to come. Dinah had been mildly surprised to be invited, since Marc seemed to be making a point of avoiding her, especially after the incident with Hassert. He had, she suspected, decided that he was going to protect her from her association with him, whether she wanted his protection or not.

"Are you sure Waterfront Park is the best place to watch?" Court fidgeted.

"We're sure," Marc said firmly. "Why don't you get out and walk around?"

"Instead of bugging you?" Court grinned. "Okay."

"Stay where I can see you," Marc warned.

"Chill, Dad." Court got out, grinning, and walked off toward the water.

Now it seemed Marc's turn to be jittery. He drummed his fingers on the steering wheel. The problem was that he was alone with her. He didn't want to be.

She struggled for the right words. How to do what she'd intended to do the next time she was alone with him? She had to do something to restore a normal relationship with Marc. They couldn't go on this way.

Her fault, she supposed. She'd let him see too clearly that she had feelings for him, and now he was torn between warning her off and protecting her.

"Maybe we ought to get out." Marc reached for the door handle.

"Wait a second." She took a steadying

breath. If she let him get out now, she'd probably never muster up the courage to do it. "I need to talk with you."

He gave her a polite, noncommittal look. "Of course."

Her heart winced. He looked at her as if she were a stranger.

"I was a little surprised that you invited me tonight."

He blinked. "I don't know what you mean."

"Let's not pretend, Marc." It took an effort to keep her voice even. "We need to clear the air between us. You've been shutting me out."

He didn't deny it. "This has turned more difficult than I expected. I don't want to expose you to any more episodes like the one with Hassert."

"The situation with Hassert is cleared up."

"That doesn't mean something else won't go wrong." His jaw set with characteristic stubbornness. "I can't protect you all the time."

"I don't want you to protect me." Shouting at him would probably do no good, although she was tempted. "I'm all grown up, Marc. You have to stop thinking of me as a child."

His eyes seemed to darken. "I don't.

Maybe that's part of the problem."

She caught back a gasp. That was more honesty than she'd expected. Or wanted. But maybe that was what was needed, that they be honest about their relationship.

"Something happened between us the other night — connection, attraction — I'm not sure what it was." She said the words slowly, feeling her way. "I didn't intend to bring that up. I know it makes you uncomfortable."

"That's not quite the word I'd pick," he said drily.

She fought the longing to jump out of the car. "I've done a great job of protecting myself since Annabel's death, you know. Keeping everything on the surface, never letting myself look too deeply. I told myself that was my way of dealing with grief."

It hadn't just been the grief. She was beginning to see that now. It was her relationship with other people, with her job, even with God. One thing to recognize it, but another to figure out what to do with it.

"I just want you to know —"

"Don't!" His voice was harsh enough to make her wince. "Look, Dinah, we both know we can't be anything to each other than what we were."

She hadn't expected anything more, but

his bluntness hurt more than it should. She swallowed the pain.

"I know that. But I'd like to think we can still be friends."

He wasn't looking at her. He was staring out the windshield, as if he saw something fascinating out on the moving water. "We'll always be friends, Dinah."

That sounded like a farewell. Her heart squeezed painfully in her chest. Friends.

Court came darting toward the car, his face excited. Maybe the boats had appeared. She could leave the car and put some space between herself and Marc.

"Dad, hey, Dad." Court wrenched the door open. "I saw him, that gardener guy you showed me the picture of."

Marc was already out of the car before she had a chance to react. "Where? Are you sure?"

She slid out her side of the car and hurried around to them.

"Over that way," Court pointed toward the crowd. "Sure, I'm sure. I looked at the picture, didn't I?"

Marc exchanged glances with her. "Let's have a look. You two stay together, will you?"

"Dad —"

"I want someone with Dinah," Marc said quickly.

"Oh. Right." Court subsided.

This time she didn't protest. Marc's expression had told her this was as much for Court's sake as for hers.

"Show me where you saw him." She refrained from taking Court's arm. He wouldn't appreciate that.

"This way." He plunged into the crowd, squirming through enthusiastically.

She followed with a bit less enthusiasm. Court was still a child, although he'd resent that furiously. He didn't remember his mother's death, and this whole business was more like a treasure hunt to him than anything else.

She grabbed his jacket to slow down his progress. "If you knock someone into the water, you're going to be extremely unpopular."

"He was standing right here." He nodded to the low railing that separated the walkway from the river. "Do you think he knows we're after him?"

"That could be." Carr was being awfully elusive, for someone who'd hinted he had information to sell. "What was he wearing?"

The act of putting a description into words would blur the image of the man in Court's mind, but that couldn't be helped. It was the constant dilemma facing police officers in dealing with eyewitnesses.

"Faded jeans. Some kind of a dark jacket, maybe a windbreaker. I didn't notice the clothes so much. I just saw his face, and I knew it was the face in the picture Dad showed me."

She nodded, looking around. The crowd was thickening now, pressing toward the water, craning for the first glimpse of the lighted boats. "I don't think we're going to find him in this crush. Let's see if your dad had any luck."

But when they'd worked their way back through the crowd to Marc's side, he shook his head. "If he was here, he may have spotted us and slipped away."

"I should've gone after him myself, instead of coming for you."

Marc slung his arm around Court's shoulders. "You did the right thing. I never want you to do something like that on your own."

"You think he's dangerous? That maybe he's the one?"

"No, I don't." Marc spoke quickly. "He acts like he knows something, but that could just be an excuse to get money."

"Maybe he figures if he's hard to get, it'll raise the price," Court said.

"That's good thinking. It could be exactly what's on his mind. If so, he'll show up

202

sooner or later." He squeezed Court's shoulders. "Don't worry about it, okay?"

"Right. Hey, look! The boats are coming." Forgetting the subject that quickly, Court pushed forward with the rest of the crowd.

She glanced at Marc's face. "Is that really what you think about Carr?"

"I don't know what I think." His voice had an edge of frustration. "But he can't stay out of sight forever." He took her arm. "Let's catch up with Court, before he ends up in the river."

Marc seemed able to dismiss Carr from his mind nearly as fast as Court did. They joined Court, who peppered them with questions as the boats, strung with lights and with Christmas music playing, began to pass by. They'd go down to the point, then up the Ashley on the other side of the peninsula, celebrating the holidays in a uniquely Charleston manner.

It was exactly like a dozen other Christmas boat parades she'd attended. But she hadn't felt this uneasiness at any of the others. She moved her shoulders, trying to shake off the sense of someone watching her.

Someone could well be watching her, but that didn't mean that person had ill feelings toward her. At least half of Charleston seemed to be here. She'd already seen a number of people she knew in the crowd. Likely the other half was down at the Battery, waiting for the boats to reach them.

A tourist, apparently feeling that Marc sounded like a native, asked him a question, and Marc turned away to answer the man. She looked around for Court. He'd moved close to the edge of the walkway, craning his neck for the best possible view of the boats.

He shouldn't be that close to the edge, although he'd dispute that if she told him so. Marc was already several paces away as the crowd ebbed and flowed between them. It was like being caught in the tide out at Sullivan's Island, thinking you knew where you were only to discover you'd moved with the current.

Instinct sent her toward Court. If he leaned out any farther, she'd grab him as if he were a two-year-old, whether he liked it or not.

She worked her way closer, frustrated by the crowd, which seemed to sense her desire and want to thwart it. She squeezed between two very large women who were engaged in a loud conversation about their Christmas shopping. Ignoring their annoyed looks, she spurted through like a cork popping from a bottle. A few more steps and she'd reach Court.

A white yacht, ablaze with lights, let forth a blast of Christmas music. The crowd pushed forward. Court, caught off guard, seemed to lose his balance, tipping forward toward the dark water.

Panic shoved her toward him. "Court!" She grabbed, her hand catching his jacket as he flailed on the edge. For an instant that seemed like an eternity they counterbalanced each other, but her feet were slipping on the damp surface and in a second they'd both be in the water —

"Hey, look out!"

Strong hands grabbed her arm, hauling her backward. Her fingers slipped on Court's jacket, but it was okay, someone else had him and he was safe.

"You okay, ma'am?"

"I'm fine. Thank you." *Thank You.* She managed to breathe again. "Court, are you all right?"

He nodded, white-faced but composed. "Yes. Sorry. Thank you, sir."

"Anytime."

Their rescuer faded back into the crowd, the whole incident over in less than a minute, probably unnoticed by most of the bystanders. Court was fine. Even if he'd fallen in, he'd have been all right — chilled from the dunking, but all right. There was no reason for the fear that snaked through her as she pulled Court close.

"You're sure you're all right?"

He nodded, not pulling away. "Let's find Dad." He looked at her, his eyes wide. "Dinah, I didn't just fall. Somebody pushed me."

ELEVEN

"Thanks, Glory." Dinah accepted the mug of coffee Marc's housekeeper handed her, sinking down on the leather couch in the family room. The Christmas tree lights were turned on, in spite of the sunshine that poured through the tall windows. Obviously Court didn't intend to miss a minute of the holiday.

"Mr. Marc will be down directly." Glory hesitated, as if she had a mind to say something more, but then she turned and went out.

That was just as well. Dinah had no wish to rehash the events of the previous evening. She'd already done that for too much of the night.

She wasn't sure she'd ever felt quite that absolutely visceral response of terror when she'd thought Court was in danger. And although she and Marc had taken turns playing it lightly in front of Court, she hadn't stopped shaking inside for hours.

She hadn't realized how much Court had come to mean to her. Oh, she'd known she loved him, of course. But that absolute terror for him was something she'd never experienced before. It must be what a mother felt when her child was in danger.

Her mind flickered briefly to Teresa's mother, to that look she had of simply waiting for something too dreadful to describe to descend on her little family. She would understand.

Annabel would understand. Would she resent Dinah for feeling that way about Court?

She wrapped her fingers around the mug, taking comfort in its warmth. Surely not. Annabel would want them to be close, wouldn't she? To her horror, she didn't know the answer to that. Her teenage adoration for her beautiful older cousin seemed naive to her now. How could she say what Annabel would want? She'd never known her as an adult.

Somehow, in the darkest hour of the night, her prayers for Court had crystallized something she'd been barely aware of until now. For Court, she could open her heart to God, breaking down the walls she'd erected to protect herself. For him, she could be open to the possibility of pain.

By morning, she'd known what she had to do. She had to convince Marc to take Court and go away. That was the only solution. Court had to be kept safe, even at the cost of never knowing who killed Annabel. Even at the cost of never seeing him or Marc again.

She heard the footsteps on the stairs soon enough that she could wipe away the tears that hovered and force a smile to her face by the time Marc opened the door.

"Dinah." He crossed to the table, pouring a mug of coffee from the carafe Glory had put there. "I need this." He turned, his gaze raking her face, and then came to sit across from her in the big leather chair. "I don't need to ask how you slept. It's written all over your face."

"Don't remind me." She took a sip of the coffee, holding the mug to hide her face for a moment. "How is Court this morning?"

"He's fine. Top of the world, in fact. Apparently nearly falling in the Cooper River was worth about a hundred e-mails to his friends." He jerked his head toward the study. "That's where he is now, in fact."

"I'm glad he's so resilient." Too bad she wasn't. "Is he still convinced someone pushed him?"

"Yes." He examined his coffee. "He could be mistaken. It could have just been the normal movement of the crowd. There were plenty of people there, and you can't always account for what a crowd will do."

She'd like to believe that. "I know. They could have surged forward accidentally, throwing Court off balance. But you don't believe that, do you?"

"No." His face tightened. "I don't. I think someone meant it for a warning. To tell me that Charleston's a dangerous place for anyone connected to me."

"That's what I think, too." She took a breath, trying to stifle the pain. "So I think you and Court should leave."

"Run away?" His eyebrows lifted.

"I don't care what you call it." She set the mug on the coffee table. The caffeine had stopped helping. "You can't risk Court's safety."

"I've been trying to convince him to go to a friend's place for the holiday. I promised I'd join him for Christmas." His smile flickered, but it held no amusement. "You'd think I could force him to go, wouldn't you?"

"Well, not unless you wanted to drag him onto the plane. He won't go unless you do, is that it?"

He nodded.

"Then you have to go, Marc." She leaned forward, as if her intensity could convince him if her words didn't. "You don't have a choice."

She couldn't read what his dark eyes were hiding. "That's what you've wanted from the moment you heard we were coming, isn't it?"

"No. Well, maybe at first." She struggled to remember how she'd felt about Marc's arrival just a few short weeks ago. "I didn't want to confront the past. I thought —" She shook her head. "It doesn't matter. Everything has changed. But you still have to admit that leaving is the only sensible thing to do."

"For Court's sake."

"Yes, of course." She'd love to know what was behind the mask he seemed to be wearing. "You can't let Court be in danger."

"No. You're right." He looked very tired all of a sudden. "We'll have to go."

The door opened on his words, and Glory came in. "There was a message for you, Mr. Marc." She held out a slip of paper. "It was that man we were talking about. Jasper Carr."

"What?" Marc lunged from the chair, snatching the piece of paper. "Why didn't you call me to the phone?"

"He didn't want me to." Glory's brow furrowed. "I don't like that man. Never did. He insisted I just give you a message." She nodded toward the paper. "Come to that address today at five. He'd meet you there."

"Was that all he said?" The question shot out in what she thought of as Marc's prosecutor voice.

"There was one other thing." She sounded reluctant.

"Let me guess. He wants me to come alone."

Glory shook her head. "Just the opposite. Said he didn't want to see you alone. He'll only meet you if Miz Dinah comes, too."

He did not want Dinah to go with him to meet Jasper Carr. And since arguing with her on the subject had done no good whatsoever, he was simply going to leave without her. He'd rather deal with the consequences of her anger than put her at any further risk, no matter how slight.

He walked quickly toward the garage. There was no doubt she'd be angry. Shy little Dinah had grown up, and the feelings he'd begun to have for her reflected that.

That didn't bear dwelling on. He couldn't explore any feeling for Dinah other than cousinly affection. Even if it hadn't been for the barriers created by the suspicion attached to him, it was impossible. No matter how she might try to break free, Dinah was tied by the past. She had idolized Annabel in a way that couldn't let her feel anything for him without a boatload of guilt.

As for him — well, Court had to come first for him. He couldn't even think about any relationship that could affect that. Court loved Dinah as a cousin, but that didn't mean he'd welcome a romantic attachment between her and his father.

He rounded the corner by the garage and came to a stop. Dinah, hugging her black leather jacket close to her body, stood waiting by the car.

"You're here." Well, that was certainly mastering the obvious.

"Somehow I thought you might decide to do this without me." She put her hand on the door handle. "It won't work, Marc. You should know that."

He glared at her over the roof of the car. "I don't know any such thing. And I don't intend to take you with me to see a character like Jasper Carr."

She yanked open the door. "Then you'd better be ready to throw me out of the car, because I'm going." She slid into the passenger seat.

Fuming wasn't doing much good. And his anger had to be at least partially frustration over the complex feelings she generated in him.

He got into the car, shut the door and fastened his seat belt. "Satisfied?"

She smiled. "I am, thank you."

He turned the ignition and began to back out of the garage. "And don't try the demure Southern belle routine on me, either. It doesn't fit with your sheer stubbornness."

"Southern ladies are always stubborn. How else would they deal with Southern men?"

"An unanswerable question." He turned out onto the street. "Do you know anything about the address Carr gave?"

"Only that it's in a neighborhood where I don't spend much time."

"All the more reason why you shouldn't be going."

She gave an elaborate sigh. "You know perfectly well why I'm going. It's not that I have any burning desire to talk to that man again, but he won't meet with you unless I'm there."

He glanced at her, to see her forehead wrinkle. "Wondering why?"

She nodded. "I can't imagine, unless for

some strange reason he thinks a second person should witness your meeting. But that doesn't make much sense."

"It does if he's afraid of me." He voiced the thought that had been in the back of his mind since he'd heard Carr's terms. "If he thinks I'm a murderer, he won't want to be alone with me."

"That's ridiculous." Dinah's voice was as sharp as he'd ever heard it. "If the man knows anything at all about what happened that night, he certainly knows it wasn't you."

"Why, Dinah?" He looked at her, his hands tightening on the wheel.

She blinked. "Why what?"

"I didn't realize, until I came back, how many people are convinced I killed Annabel. But not you. Why aren't you afraid to be alone with me?"

"Well, I — I just know you too well. I know you couldn't do anything of the kind."

"That's not really an answer and you know it." He wasn't sure why it was so important to him to press her. "You were a kid then. You took me at face value."

"If you mean I took you for granted — of course I did. You were part of my family."

"Maybe you didn't know me as well as you thought you did. What does any sixteen-year-old know about the adults around her?"

"I'm not sixteen any longer. And I'm still sure." She shook her head, and he saw the fluid movement of her hair, blue-black against the black leather of the jacket. "Some things a person is just sure of. I don't have to analyze my feelings. I know."

"You were there that night." He paused for a heartbeat, praying he was saying the right thing. "Maybe you're sure about me for another reason."

She didn't speak, but he saw her hands clench together in her lap.

He had to keep trying. "Dinah, you had a head injury that night. You know as well as I do that sometimes people can't remember the things that happened moments or even hours before an accident like that."

"There's nothing to remember." Her voice was tight and strained. "I didn't see anything that night. I didn't."

He wanted to probe, to ask if she remembered coming out of her room, starting down the stairs. Something had made her fall. Surely that wasn't a coincidence.

But gut instinct told him he'd driven her as far as he dared for the time being. They'd come back to it again. They had to.

He checked the street sign and then pulled

slowly to the curb. "This is it. Not very prepossessing, is it?"

The house had once probably been a charming Victorian single-family home. Now shutters hung lopsided, paint peeled, and a general aura of decay surrounded the place. Like so many houses of this era, it had been chopped up into small apartments. Presumably Carr lived in one of them or imposed on a friend who did.

Dinah's hand was already on the door handle. He reached across her to still the movement, bringing his face very close to hers.

Too close. He drew back a little. "Stay in the car, Dinah. Please."

"I don't think Carr will interpret staying in the car as coming with you." She pulled the handle up. "Let's get this over with."

The doorbell didn't seem to produce any sound, but the double doors, their etched glass now grimy and cracked, stood open. He stepped into the hall, motioning Dinah to stay behind him.

Silence, nothing but silence. Either the other apartments were vacant, or the tenants were extremely quiet. He started up the narrow stairwell, which probably replaced something that had once been grander. According to Carr's directions, he was on the second floor.

He felt Dinah close behind him. She wasn't putting her hand on the filthy railing, and he could hardly blame her.

"I'm having a bad feeling about this." He hadn't intended to whisper, but the silence around them seemed to suppress any noise. "Dinah, please go back outside, at least until I see if he's here."

Her fingers closed on his jacket sleeve. "If you think I'm waiting down there by myself, you'd best think again."

"Stubborn," he muttered, and quickened his pace. As she'd said, let's get this over with.

The door to 203 stood slightly open. "Carr? Jasper Carr, are you here? It's Marc Devlin."

Nothing. He glanced at Dinah. Her eyes were wide in the gloom.

"Carr?" He tapped on the door, and it swung open.

It took him a moment to register what he was seeing. Carr lay on a couch, legs sprawled half off. A bottle had fallen from one hand to the floor.

"He's drunk," he said, disgust in his voice. And then something about the stillness, the rigidity of the body, began to penetrate. "Stay here," he ordered Dinah, trusting that his tone left no room for argument.

He crossed the room until he stood staring down at the man. Reluctantly he put his fingers on Carr's throat, searching for a pulse. There was none. Whatever Carr had intended to tell him, he'd never hear now. The man was dead.

Dinah sat in the captain's office at police headquarters, not sure how long she'd been there. Long enough, at any rate, for the shaking to subside.

She took a steadying breath and then raised the foam cup of coffee to her lips. It was just as bitter as Tracey always insisted, but it did serve to warm her.

She found Tracey studying her. "This really is bad coffee." She tried to keep her voice light, tried to erase the worry that clouded Tracey's face.

"If I'd had more time, I'd have stopped for some of the good stuff." Tracey ran her hand through her hair in a characteristic gesture. "You feel any better?"

She nodded. She and Marc had been separated from the moment they'd arrived at headquarters. She'd been shown into the office, and Tracey had been hauled in to take her statement, probably out of deference to her status as a civilian police employee.

Marc had been shown no such consideration. He was in an interview room with Draydon. She could only hope he'd remembered his own training and refused to say anything until he called an attorney.

She shifted in the hard metal chair. "How can Draydon possibly think Marc had anything to do with Carr's death?" She shouldn't put Tracey on the spot, but she couldn't hold the question back. "I was with him when we found Carr. Or does he think I was involved?"

"Of course not. He doesn't know that it was murder. He's just trying to cover all the bases, that's all. I'm sure you'll both be free to leave soon."

Did Tracey really believe that, or was she trying to make her feel better?

"There was a pill bottle open next to him." She was driven to talk about it, even if Tracey couldn't respond. "It could have been an accidental overdose."

"We'll know more about it after the autopsy." Tracey surveyed the outer office, as if hoping someone would come to rescue her.

"Or it could have been suicide." Maybe the coffee was doing some good. Her mind seemed to be working again. "If it was, isn't that as good as an admission of guilt? Carr must have killed Annabel."

Tracey hitched her chair closer. "Listen, Dinah, you know I can't talk about it."

"I know." She reached out impulsively and grasped her friend's hand. "I know you're just here because we work together." A thought struck her, taking her breath away. "Or is that all over? Will they refuse to give me any more work because of my involvement in this case?"

"I won't lie to you, Dinah. It's not going to do you any good around here, at least not unless this business is cleared up quickly."

"So I'm persona non grata, is that it?" There was more bitterness than the coffee would produce. All the work she'd done to be accepted here was going to go for nothing.

"Look, don't worry about it this early in the game." She gripped her hand. "You know I'm not giving up on you."

"Thanks, Tracey." She shouldn't burden Tracey with her troubles. It wasn't fair to her, when there was nothing she could do.

"Let's talk about something else." Tracey sounded determinedly cheerful. "How was your aunt holding up when you talked to her?"

She'd called Aunt Kate the moment she'd been allowed to, afraid she'd hear something on the radio or television and panic.

"She surprised me, actually." She noted the sad-looking artificial Christmas tree on the corner of the captain's desk. "I tend to forget how strong she is. Just because she's physically weak now doesn't mean she's lost any of that moral fortitude. She has Court with her, and he'll stay there until we get back. She and Alice are teaching him to make taffy, whether he wants to or not."

"I can imagine how a teenage boy is reacting to that." Tracey smiled. "Your aunt —" The door opened.

Dinah's breath caught. It was Marc. "What happened? Are you all right?"

Tracey rose. "I'll just leave you alone for a few minutes." She went out, closing the door behind her.

Marc shook his head, his face grim. "It's hard to tell what Draydon thinks. He's predisposed to be suspicious of me, obviously." He sank into the chair Tracey had vacated. "I can't say I blame him. I'd react in the same way if it were my case."

"Unless he wants to believe I was in on it, he can't believe you harmed Carr. I was with you."

He shook his head, leaning forward but not touching her. "It's not that simple, sugar." The endearment seemed to slip out without his noticing it. "I don't know what the coroner will say, but Carr had been dead for a while. They could conclude that I killed him earlier and then came back with you, hoping that would allay suspicion."

"That's ridiculous." Anger warmed her. "Draydon's thinking is too convoluted for a police detective if he thinks that."

He shrugged. "Well, let's look on the bright side. I didn't see a note, but that doesn't mean there wasn't one. If Carr committed suicide it will go a long way toward clearing me, even if he didn't leave a note." He reached out, his fingers closing over hers. "I just wish you hadn't been there. Aunt Kate will scalp me for involving you."

"Aunt Kate is fine. She —" The door opened again, and suddenly her heart raced.

Draydon stood in the doorway. Marc straightened, dropping her hand and rising.

"Did you want to talk with me again?"

Draydon looked as if he'd like to say yes, but instead he shook his head. "You and Ms. Westlake are free to go. For the moment."

She stood, grabbing her jacket, only too

glad to get out before he changed his mind. But Marc hadn't moved. His jaw tightened.

"What does that mean?" He sliced off the question.

Draydon held the door politely. "The investigation has a long way to go. You should know that, Counselor. But I'm guessing we'll find that Carr knew something about your wife's death and was foolish enough to try and blackmail a murderer."

Marc shouldn't say anything. She grabbed his arm, her fingers digging in.

"You heard him, Marc. Let's go home." She tugged him toward the door, breathing a little easier when she got him past Draydon.

"Just one thing." Draydon dropped the words as they passed him. When they both looked at him, he smiled.

"Don't leave town," he said gently. "Either of you."

TWELVE

Dinah's steps slowed as she and Marc approached Aunt Kate's front door. She paused, looking up at him. "Maybe we'd both best take a minute to put a smile on."

He lifted an eyebrow. "Do you honestly think we'll fool anyone?"

"I don't know." Her heart twisted at the thought of Aunt Kate's frailty. "But we have to try and keep Aunt Kate from realizing how serious the situation is. She gets so frightened for me."

His hand closed over hers. "She loves you. You're all she has."

"I know." She shivered as a breeze ruffled her hair, rustling the leaves of the hundred-year-old live oak they stood under. "She's all the family I have, too."

"We're family." His fingers tightened almost painfully. "Court and I. Even if we're not Westlakes."

Family. However much he might deny it,

she was still Annabel's little cousin to him. "I know."

"It's probably best if Court doesn't know all the details either," he said. "The difficulty will be keeping them from him. He's very resourceful. If I don't answer his questions, he'll look up the newspaper on the Internet."

She had to smile at that. "I suppose he would, wouldn't he? Well, all we can do is try."

They stepped onto the piazza, and he reached for the door handle. "Odd, isn't it? My decision to leave town came just a little too late. Now we can't."

Draydon's words seemed to hang in the air. *Don't leave town, either of you.*

Well, she had no intention of going anywhere, but Marc and Court should be safe back in Boston by now. The thought left an empty feeling where her heart should be. Sooner or later they'd leave, and she'd have to learn to get along without them. It wouldn't be easy.

Marc opened the door, and they stepped into the warm hallway, lush with a sweet aroma. Court plunged from the parlor to meet them.

"Hey, are you guys okay? What happened? Did you do CPR on the guy?"

Marc sent her a despairing glance over his son's head. "Yes, we're all right. No, we didn't." He wrapped his arm around Court's shoulders. "Listen, son, we don't want to upset Aunt Kate. Let's try not to talk about it just now."

Court's face was eloquent in his disappointment. "Bummer."

"Okay?" Marc prodded.

"Okay. But I think Aunt Kate's really getting a secret thrill out of it, even though she was worried about Dinah."

"Well, let's go in and assure her that Dinah's fine." He gave Court a quick hug before releasing him. "I'll talk to you about it later. Promise."

"Dinah?" Aunt Kate's voice wavered just a little. "Come in, please."

She hurried into the parlor, pinning a smile on her face. "I'm sorry, Aunt Kate." She bent to press her cheek against Aunt Kate's. "It took forever. I hope you didn't worry too much."

Her aunt's hand caught hers and clung, but she managed to smile. "Court did a wonderful job of explaining that naturally you'd have to tell the police everything you saw. I hope it wasn't too dreadful."

"Not at all." She hoped she'd be forgiven the small lie to save her aunt distress.

"Goodness, it smells as if you all have been cooking up a storm. What did you make?" She addressed the question to Court, who grinned.

"They taught me how to make taffy. And then Alice and I made about a million of those little pecan cookies. 'Course I probably ate about half of them."

"No such thing," Alice said. She stood in the doorway, smiling at him. Court had obviously made a conquest. Alice didn't let just anyone into her kitchen. "You come and help me carry the trays in. Your daddy and Dinah must be starving."

"We don't need . . ." she began, but it was too late. Feeding people was Alice's way of coping. Well, it would keep Court busy, anyway. She glanced at Marc, suspecting that he was thinking the same.

He moved around the parlor, as if too restless to sit still after the events of the past few hours. He stopped by the mantel.

"I see you've done some more Christmas decorating. I remember these angels from years ago."

Startled, Dinah looked at the mantel. There, tucked among the greens, were Aunt Kate's Christmas angels, fragile china figures dating from a century ago at least.

"We haven't gotten the angels out in years.

You always say they're too fragile."

Aunt Kate gave a little shrug, the lacy shawl she had around her shoulders moving against her green wool dress. "I thought it would amuse Court. And he's very dextrous, for a boy."

"I didn't break a thing." Court came in from the kitchen, carrying a tray with the coffee service.

"See that you don't start with the Meissen china," Alice said. She began putting plates of cookies, savories, and tiny sandwiches on the coffee table.

"Alice, that's far too much food."

"Speak for yourself, Cousin Dinah." Court snatched a chicken salad sandwich. "I'm a growing boy."

"Leave some for the rest of us," Marc said. "It's not often I get to have some of Alice's shrimp paste, and I'm sure it's still the best in Charleston."

Alice beamed. "I'll just bring out some of that hot chocolate young Courtney likes. Dinah, you should drink it, too. Better for you than coffee."

"I suppose it's pointless to tell you I'm one of the grown-ups," she said.

Alice paused in the archway, turning to deliver a parting shot. "You're not so grown-up as all that."

"Alice, you're under the kissing ball." Court grinned, putting his arm around her and kissing her cheek.

Alice swatted him, but her eyes glowed with laughter. "Just for that, you come along and carry the hot chocolate in."

"That boy," Aunt Kate said indulgently. "He spotted the kissing ball in one of the boxes and wanted to know what it was. Nothing would do but that he hang it up right away."

"I hope he didn't tire you out." Marc bent over to take one of the delicate china cups Aunt Kate held out to him. "It was good of you to have him here."

"Of course he'd come here," she said. "We're family."

There that word was again. Family. Aunt Kate would never see Marc as anything but Annabel's husband, and there was no changing that.

Well, at least the crises of the past few days seemed to have mended whatever reserve she'd held on to against Marc. She was treating him as she always had.

Court came back in with the hot chocolate and solemnly poured a cup for Dinah. As he bent to hand it to her, he grinned. "I'll get you some coffee, if you'd rather."

"You'd better not disobey Alice. She

always gets her way. Although judging by that kiss, you've already figured out a way to her good side."

"You don't think she minded, do you?" His face grew serious. "I just wanted to distract Aunt Kate. I wouldn't want to upset Alice."

What a kind heart he had. "Court, no one could be upset at a kiss from you."

He seized her hands in his. "Then it's your turn, Cousin Dinah." He tugged her, laughing, under the kissing ball and planted a noisy kiss on her cheek.

She hugged him, smiling. She'd told Marc they mustn't upset Court and Aunt Kate, but it was really Court who'd managed to cheer everyone.

"Come on, Dad." Court grabbed his father's arm. "You have to give Dinah a kiss, too." He shoved him toward her.

A wave of panic swept through her when Court pushed them together. Marc's arms closed around her. He couldn't kiss her here, like this, in front of everyone. She looked up, hoping Marc would turn it away with a laugh.

But the laughter in his face seemed to slip away as he looked at her. His eyes darkened.

She was suspended in the moment, unable to speak, to move, to do anything to turn away the inevitable. Marc bent, it seemed in slow motion, and his lips found hers.

The kiss couldn't have lasted more than a few seconds, but truth could be seen in the momentary flash of lightning.

They'd managed to distract Court and Aunt Kate from the danger, but at what cost? She couldn't deny what she felt for Marc any longer, at least not to herself. She was in love with him, and there was no future in that at all.

"Dinah?" Aunt Kate called her name as soon as she came downstairs the next morning. "Is that you?"

"Of course." She hurried into the breakfast room, giving Aunt Kate a reassuring hug. "Who else would it be at this hour of the morning?"

"I'm being silly, I suppose." Aunt Kate fumbled with her teaspoon. "I just wanted to be sure you're all right."

"I'm fine." She poured a cup of tea and helped herself to a piece of toast. She didn't really feel like eating, but Aunt Kate and Alice would worry themselves to death if she didn't.

"You had a terrible experience." Tears glistened in her eyes. "I know all of you tried to make light of it, but it must have been dreadful, finding that man. Marc never should have taken you there."

"He didn't want to. I didn't give him a choice." If only there was something she could say that would allay Aunt Kate's fears. But she was afraid, too. Afraid for Marc, with the cloud of suspicion hanging over him. Afraid for Court, who must not face losing his father.

"I always thought Annabel was the stubborn one." Her aunt dabbed at her eyes with a lacy handkerchief. "You've changed since Marc came back."

"Don't think that." She put her hand over her aunt's. "I'm the same person I've always been. It's just that having to face things about Annabel's death has made me more — aware, I guess. Responsible."

"You've always been too responsible. Too serious. Even that summer, trying to take over with Courtney when Annabel —" She choked.

Dinah patted her, alarmed. "Don't, darling. Don't upset yourself this way. It's going to be all right."

Even to soothe Aunt Kate, she couldn't seem to make that sound terribly convincing. How was it going to be all right? What if Marc were charged? Her feelings were of small concern next to that very real possibility.

"No. It isn't." The strength in her aunt's voice startled her. "I failed. I failed Annabel. And you."

"Don't be silly. You've always been there when I needed you."

Aunt Kate gripped her hand with feverish intensity. "I should never have sent you away. I thought I was doing the right thing, but now I know it was wrong. We should have faced it together."

"You did your best. That's all anyone can do."

Aunt Kate had probably kept herself up most of the night, worrying herself into this state.

"I failed you both." She shook her head. "Even with Annabel right across the street, I couldn't keep her from grief."

"What happened wasn't your fault. It wasn't anyone's fault except the person who did it."

Her head moved tremulously from side to side. "I knew, you see." Her voice was hardly more than a whisper. "And I didn't confront her. I should have, but I was afraid. I didn't want to lose her."

"What are you talking about, Aunt Kate?

What did you know? Something about An-nabel?"

Her heart was suddenly beating in sharp, quick thuds, and she couldn't seem to get her breath.

Aunt Kate covered her face with her palms. "I knew, and I did nothing."

She didn't want to hear, didn't want to know. If Aunt Kate had been afraid, she was, too. She didn't want to know.

But she had to. For Marc's sake, and Court's.

She took her aunt's hands gently in hers, drawing them away from her face. "It's all right. Really, it is. Just tell me about it, and I'll take care of it."

Tears spilled quietly onto Aunt Kate's cheeks. "It was Annabel. That summer. I heard her. There was another man. She was seeing another man."

Her throat was so tight she couldn't possibly push any words out. But she had to. "Are you sure?"

"Yes." It was the barest whisper. "I'm sure. I heard her, talking to him on the phone. Her voice — it couldn't have been anything else."

She couldn't think, just yet, of all that implied. "She didn't know you heard her?"

"No. I slipped away. I should have confronted her. If I had, maybe it wouldn't have happened."

"You mustn't think that. There's no way of knowing. Talking to her about it might have made things even worse." Although how they could be worse, she didn't know. "Who was he? The man. Who was it?" Dread gripped her heart.

"I don't know. I never knew. I never heard his voice. Just Annabel's."

"You didn't have a guess?" She'd been an oblivious sixteen-year-old who'd seen nothing, even when it was right under her nose. But Aunt Kate had been an elderly woman, who'd surely seen enough of life to notice something — a look, a word.

"I didn't know. I didn't want to know. I thought I could pretend not to know. But it was so hard. And when Marcus came back —"

Marc. What was she going to tell Marc?

Aunt Kate pressed her hands. "You have to take care of it, Dinah. I can't. You have to decide whether or not to tell Marcus, because I can't."

He shouldn't have kissed Dinah. Marc moved restlessly around the house the next day, unable to settle to anything for very long. With everything else he had to worry about, he seemed fixated on that moment.

He'd expected to dream about finding Carr's body. Instead his dreams had been impossible ones of holding Dinah, laughing, kissing, with nothing to shadow their happiness. Impossible dreams.

He rechecked the locks on the back door and the cellar door. Court had to be safe. Draydon's demand not to leave town didn't apply to Court, so he could send him to friends. But if he did, he wouldn't be with him to protect him.

And Dinah — he rubbed the back of his neck, where tension had taken up residence. Dinah had to be kept safe, too. Being around him had endangered her. If she had any sense, she'd steer clear of him. But since even now he could see her approaching the front door, that seemed unlikely.

He flung the door open, torn between his need to be with her and his conviction that she was safer away from him. "What brings you here?"

Dinah blinked and walked past him into the hallway. "What a gracious greeting. I'm fine, thanks, and you?"

"Sorry." He had manners enough left to be embarrassed. "I'm afraid being suspected of yet another murder has eroded any Southern courtesy I had left."

Her brows drew together. "You don't really think that, do you?"

"Draydon didn't tell me not to leave town because he likes having me around."

"He told me that, too, but I don't interpret it to mean that he suspects me of murder."

"No. He just thinks you might be a witness." He gave in to the temptation to grasp her hand. "I'm sorry, Dinah. I never should have involved you in this."

"Seems to me I involved myself." She glanced toward the stairwell at the sound of several loud thumps. "What on earth is Court doing now?"

"Rummaging around the attic, I suppose. It's his current fascination. He appears periodically to announce a new Christmas decoration project, or to suggest that some other piece of furniture be brought down. He'd have everything out if we were here long enough."

"I suppose it will all have to be gone through, in any event. Where are you putting things?" She turned around, as if expecting to see furniture piled in the hallway.

"We brought the table down to the dining room. Court decided he needed it for some project he has in mind. And the drop-leaf desk that used to be in Annabel's room intrigued him. We put that in the front parlor." His voice became dry when he had to refer to the room where Annabel died.

Dinah seemed to become aware that he was still holding her hand and drew it away, her face composed. She did a better job of ignoring the currents between them than he did.

Or maybe that meant she was retreating, pulling that wall around herself again. If so, it was something else for which he was to blame.

"It almost sounds as if Court has decided to stay."

"I don't think it's that, exactly. Usually he tells me what he's thinking, but not this time."

"Has he asked you anything about what Draydon suspects?" Her eyes darkened with worry.

"No, but he's a smart kid. He's bound to figure out something is going on." He rubbed the back of his neck again. It didn't help.

"Marc, we need to talk —"

Court's footsteps thudded down the stairs. "Hey, I didn't know Dinah was here. Hi, Dinah." He swung around the newel post at the bottom. "You didn't bring any more cookies, did you?"

"Court," he said warningly.

His son grinned, unrepentant. "It's a compliment, Dad. Dinah knows that."

"I'll tell Alice," Dinah said. "I'm sure she'll send a care package over."

"Come on, I want you both to see what I set up in the dining room." He swung the door open. "I found Dad's old train set."

"I didn't know that's what you were up to." He followed Dinah into the dining room. "So that's why you insisted we had to bring the table down."

The train set took him back to his childhood, although his mother would never have allowed him to set it up on the dining-room table. It had always gone in the playroom. He'd saved it for Court and then forgotten it when they'd left Charleston. Well, it was one thing they wouldn't forget this time.

"I waited for you to be here before I tried it." Court picked up the extension cord. "Ready?" He shoved the cord into the socket.

With a faint hiss, all the lights in the house went out. Court stared at him, chagrinned. "Oops."

He shook his head, smiling. "I had a feeling that if you plugged one more thing in, you'd blow a fuse."

"Don't feel bad," Dinah said. "At least it

happened in the daytime, when you can see to fix it."

"I'll get it, Dad."

"No, just go around and unplug a few things. I know where the new fuses are." He pushed through the swinging door to the kitchen, still smiling. Blown fuse or not, Court and the train set had distracted him for a few minutes, at least.

The drawer next to the stove held the flashlight and the fresh box of fuses. He snatched them up and headed for the cellar door. Even in the middle of the afternoon, it would be dark enough in the cellar to require a flashlight.

He could hear Dinah and Court talking in the dining room as he opened the cellar door. Dinah was good for Court. And maybe, in a way, Court was good for her, too. He'd been wrong to think keeping them apart was for the best. Regardless of what happened now, Court understood the power of family.

He switched the flashlight on, aiming it at the wooden stairs, and started down. If he —

The tread cracked beneath his foot. He lurched, off balance, reaching for something to grab, too startled even to yell. His hand closed on a water pipe, cold against his palm, and for a split second he thought he was okay.

Then the step broke, crumbling under him, his body dropping downward, his hand clenching at the pipe, slipping, losing it, knowing he was falling.

THIRTEEN

Dinah heard the crash, and for an instant she and Court stared at each other, uncomprehending. Pain flashed through her. "Marc!"

They bolted toward the cellar door, jostling each other in their hurry. Court reached the door a step ahead of her, charging through.

Instinct had her grabbing his arm before she thought through the danger. They teetered together on the tiny landing.

Daylight from the open door touched what was left of the stairs. Two steps clung to the landing. The rest of the stairway was a mass of jagged timbers.

Marc lay crumpled on the cement floor, the broken flashlight rolling away from his out-flung hand. He wasn't moving. Her heart ripped in two.

"Marc!"

"Dad!" Anguish filled Court's voice.

"Dad, say something. Please, be all right."

He leaned forward as if he'd try to jump down, and Dinah yanked him back.

"The bulkhead door. We have to go around the outside to get to him. Hurry."

She shot toward the front door, pausing just long enough to grab her cell phone from the handbag she'd left on the hall table. The mirror above it reflected her white, frightened face.

Please, Lord, please, Lord, let him be all right.

She punched in 911 as they ran, gasping out the address and the circumstances. Court reached the slanted double doors first and pulled them open, plunging down the few steps to basement level.

She followed, heart thudding in her ears. *Please, let him be all right.*

Court dropped down beside his father. "Dad, Dad!"

"Easy, Court. Take it easy." She pulled him out of the way, putting her hand on Marc's chest, and relief flooded through her.

"He's breathing." Her voice choked on the words. "He's alive. The ambulance is on its way. They'll be here in a couple of minutes. It's going to be all right."

Thank You, God. Thank You.

"How bad is he hurt?" Court was trying

244

not to cry, but his voice was choked. "Why isn't he saying anything?"

"Careful, don't bump him." She moved to touch Marc's head cautiously. "It looks as if he's knocked out." She ran her hands over his arms and legs. Nothing obviously wrong, but how did she know?

"We should get a pillow," Court said. "We can't just leave him on the floor."

"Best not to try and move him until the paramedics get here." She understood Court's urge to help. He needed to do something that would make him feel he was helping his father. "A blanket would be good, though."

Court shot to his feet. "I'll get one. Be right back." He thundered out of the cellar.

Alone with Marc, she smoothed his dark hair away from his face, allowing herself the luxury of letting a few hot tears fall.

"Be all right," she whispered. "You have to be all right, Marc. We can't get along without you."

Court ran back with the blanket just as she heard the wail of a siren. She grabbed the blanket.

"You'd better go and show them where we are."

Court nodded, his face white, and ran out again, reappearing a few seconds later with the team of paramedics.

Dinah put her arm around him, drawing him a few feet away from Marc so that they could work. "It's going to be all right," she soothed, wishing she knew that for sure. "Your dad's in good hands now. Let's go outside so they have room to work."

Nodding, Court rubbed his eyes with the back of his hands and followed her out into the chill winter sunshine. "Are you sure he's going to be all right?"

"I'm sure he is." *Please, Father.*

Neighbors had come out onto the street, and she saw Alice lingering at the gate. Dinah motioned her in, and then went to meet her halfway.

"Tell my aunt not to worry," she said quickly, before the woman could launch into a hundred questions. "Marc fell on the cellar steps. They'll probably take him to the medical center to check him out, and Court and I will go along. I'll call her from there."

Alice's eyes were bright with curiosity, but she managed not to ask anything. "Take care of that boy." She turned and hustled back out the gate.

The paramedics were bringing Marc out of the cellar on a stretcher when she reached them. She clutched Court's hand as they

followed the stretcher to the waiting ambulance. Poor kid — he didn't have anyone
but his father. No wonder he looked terrified.

She gripped his hand tighter. "He's going
to be okay, Court. You have to hang on to
that. I'll be with you the whole time. You're
not in this alone."

He nodded, tears welling in his eyes. They
reached the ambulance, and he caught one
of the paramedics by the arm.

"I want to ride with my dad."

The paramedic looked at her, as if for support. "That's not a good idea, son. We'll be
working on him."

"I'll drive us," Dinah said quickly. "We'll
follow them to the hospital."

Court shook his head. "I want to go with
him."

The paramedic was shaking his head when
Marc moved.

"Court." His voice was barely more than
a whisper, but joy shot through her at the
sound.

"Dad." Court launched himself at the
stretcher, his voice breaking.

"I'm all right. Now don't be a pest. You
ride with Dinah, you hear?"

Court nodded, clutching his father's hand.

"We'll see you there, Dad."

She understood, only too well, what Court felt. It was hard to watch Marc being slid into the ambulance, hard to see the doors close, shutting them out.

"He talked." Court turned to her, tears shimmering in his eyes. "You heard him. He talked. He's going to be okay, isn't he?"

"Of course." She forced strength into her voice. Court needed to know that he could count on her. "He's going to be fine."

She caught Court's hand as they hurried to the car, and he didn't pull away. Marc was going to be all right. She had to believe that.

She also had to know the answer to the question that hadn't seemed to occur to anyone else yet. What had made the stairs collapse when Marc was on them?

"I feel okay. I want to go home." Marc repeated the words for probably the twentieth time, this time to the attending physician in the emergency room. If he said them often enough, maybe they'd sink in.

He sat up on the narrow bed, pulling his shirt on and trying not to grimace at the pain in his bruised ribs.

The doctor raised her eyebrows. "Hurts, doesn't it? You'll really do better to let us keep you overnight, Mr. Devlin."

He managed a smile. "You wouldn't put it that way if you really thought it essential that I stay, now would you?"

"Probably not." She studied his chart, her eyes tired behind her glasses. "You're a lucky man, in my opinion. You fell eight feet onto a concrete floor and didn't break anything. Except for the bruises and a mild concussion, I can't find anything wrong."

"So I'll do fine at home." All he wanted was to get out of this sterile environment and be with Court, so he could reassure him. But he wasn't going to let his son see him lying in a hospital bed.

He clutched the edge of the bed and slid forward until he was standing on his own two feet. Maybe he wasn't a pretty sight, with bruises and abrasions down one side of his face, but at least he was upright.

The doctor sighed at his stubbornness. "All right, you can go. But only if there's a competent adult to stay with you tonight. I don't want you alone with only your son to look out for you. It's not fair to him."

"I don't need —" he began, but he didn't get any further.

"I'll stay with him and his son tonight." Dinah stood in the doorway, Court pressing behind her, his face screwed up as if he were trying not to cry. Dinah looked at the doctor, not at him. "Will that be satisfactory?"

The doctor gave her an assessing look before nodding. "I'll have the nurse give you a sheet of instructions." She went out, smiling at Court as she passed him.

He didn't want to bring Dinah in any deeper, but who else would he call? Not elderly Aunt Kate. Glory lived clear out in Monck's Corners. Phil's wife would have a fit at the thought of his helping, and as for James — well, James seemed to have tried him and found him guilty. That caused a separate small pang. He'd shut all of his Charleston connections out of his life, one way or another, and only Dinah was left.

I've involved you enough, Dinah. I don't want to risk your getting hurt. But he couldn't say any of those things in front of Court.

"The nurse said we could come in." Her glance touched his half-buttoned shirt and skittered away. "Do you need some help with that?"

He nodded. "Court, be a buddy and button this for me. My ribs feel like a linebacker has been standing on them."

Court came to him in a rush, relief washing over his face. "You're really okay?"

Marc ruffled his hair. "I'm really okay. You taking good care of Dinah?"

"Sure thing." Court busied himself with the buttons, head down. "I'm glad you're all right." His voice was husky.

"Me, too, son." He looked over Court's head at Dinah, who stood just out of reach of his hand. "Thanks, Dinah. For everything."

Tears glittered in her eyes, and she didn't attempt to hide them. "My pleasure. Just don't scare us like that again."

For a moment he couldn't look away. Close, so close. He wanted to reach out and draw her into his arms. But he couldn't. It wasn't fair.

He pushed himself away from the bed. "Look, about staying with us tonight, that's really not necessary. I'm sure we'll be fine."

"I'm sure you will, too, but that doesn't mean I'm going to leave you alone."

"I don't need a bodyguard, Dinah."

"Actually, maybe you do." She slung her bag over her shoulder. "Shall we get out of here?"

He nodded. He'd make another effort later, once Dinah saw that he could take care of himself and Court.

He took a step, winced, and threw his arm over Court's shoulder. "I guess I could use a little help."

They emerged into the waiting room.

Dinah, who was just ahead of him, stiffened suddenly, as if presented with an unwelcome sight.

He moved past her and saw that he was right. Lieutenant Draydon leaned across the registration desk, apparently arguing with the clerk. At the sight of them the quarrel stopped.

"Mr. Devlin." He approached, giving him the once-over. "Looks like you're not hurt too badly."

"I'm all right." He clipped the words off. It wasn't any of Draydon's business, and how on earth had he found out about the incident so fast, anyway? "You'll excuse me. We were just leaving."

Draydon planted himself in his path. "I have a few questions about this accident of yours."

He gritted his teeth. Probably the fastest way to get rid of the man was to give him the bare facts. "It was just that — an accident. The cellar steps gave way, and I fell."

"Nobody else in the house at the time?"

"My son. And Ms. Westlake. Why does a household accident interest the police?"

He stepped around Draydon and moved toward the exit. He shouldn't have asked that question. It was one he didn't want answered in front of Court.

"Funny, that is. How problems seem to be dogging you since you came back to Charleston," Draydon drawled. "I'd just like to know why. Call it professional curiosity. I'm sure Ms. Westlake understands."

Dinah whirled, the fury on her face startling. "No, I don't understand. Mr. Devlin is in pain. He needs to go home, not stand here answering questions."

"Now, Ms. Westlake —"

"No!" Her voice cracked like a whip. "If you want to investigate something, why don't you investigate why that step broke?"

Her words seemed to hang in the air for a long moment. Then Lieutenant Draydon leaned toward her, his whole face sharpening with interest. "Now, what makes you say that, I wonder?"

Marc grasped Dinah's arm, but he suspected she didn't need the hint to say no more. "That's all," he said shortly. "We're done here."

Ignoring Draydon, he hustled Court and Dinah out into the parking lot. They were twenty feet from the door before he realized he didn't know where the car was.

He stopped. "Sorry. I didn't mean to give you the bum's rush."

"You did the right thing." Dinah's voice shook. "I'm sorry. I shouldn't have said that.

I just —"

"I understand." He did. He understood that she cared for him, and that caring was leading her into a difficult, maybe a dangerous place. "I appreciate you defending me."

"I didn't do a very good job of it." She looked up at him, trying to smile, but her lips trembled.

Court had walked on toward the car, and for a moment they stood alone in the darkened parking lot, the faint glow from one of the overhead lights touching the upturned oval of Dinah's face.

His heart clutched. She was inexpressibly dear to him. He could never tell her that. He couldn't ask her to share the suspicion that was directed at him. And even if that were resolved, Annabel's memory would always stand between them.

He needed to lay the past to rest and push on into the future. But Dinah could never face it, so she could never let it go.

Dinah walked slowly down the staircase, running her hand along the rail. She no longer panicked on the stairs, but holding on seemed a wise precaution.

Court was asleep in his bed, oblivious to the concerns that plagued the adults in his life. His dad was safe and at home. That was all it took to give him uninterrupted slumber.

She couldn't hope for the same. In fact, she'd probably settle with a book on the sofa in the family room and stay awake for the duration. She'd be of small use to Marc if he needed her and she was asleep.

Besides, any sleep she had in this house was bound to be tortured by the dream again. A chill touched her, and she went quickly down the rest of the stairs.

"Marc?" He was supposed to be resting, but somehow she doubted it. She glanced in the family room. Empty.

"Marc?" She called again, softly. Waking Court wouldn't make this night any easier, and she had no desire to launch into reassuring him again.

Or reassuring Aunt Kate, for that matter. It had been all she could do to keep her elderly great-aunt from coming to the hospital to see for herself that everyone was all right. She'd developed a fierce, protective love for Court in the short time she'd known him.

Dinah started back down the hall to the kitchen. Maybe Marc had decided to get something to eat. She could fix him a sandwich —

She stopped, aghast. The cellar door stood

open, and Marc's legs extended into the hallway.

She reached the door in a second, terrified at what she might find. "Marc!" She clutched at his legs.

He turned an annoyed face to her. "What are you doing?"

"What are *you* doing?" Relief and anger sharpened her tone. "You're supposed to be resting. I thought you'd collapsed."

"Sorry." He shook his head and winced at the movement. "I didn't mean to scare you. I'm just following your lead."

"My lead?"

"You're the one who told Draydon he should be looking into why the stairs collapsed."

"That doesn't mean I think you should be disobeying doctor's orders. Please go and rest."

She sat on the floor next to him, trying to peer over his shoulder. With the errant fuse replaced, she had a good view of the jagged timbers and the concrete floor. A shudder went through her. The image of Marc lying there would be fodder for a few more nightmares.

Marc played the flashlight he held over what remained of the top steps. Obviously he didn't intend to come out until he'd finished what he was doing.

She didn't want to know, but she had to. "Well? How does it look?"

He slid back into the hall next to her, raising himself to a sitting position. She could see by his expression it wasn't good news.

"The stairway was pretty rickety to begin with, braced by a couple of upright supports. It looks to me as if someone sawed almost all the way through the uprights. The first time anyone put any weight on the tread, he could bet the whole thing would come down. And he could have tampered with the fuse box at the same time."

Her mind raced, trying to imagine it. "But how could anyone get into the cellar? How could they have done that without being heard?"

Marc shrugged, his face hard. "I locked the door into the cellar, but not the bulkhead doors. I figured the only danger was someone getting into the house itself. My mistake."

"You'd have heard him, surely." His expression had begun to frighten her. Not for herself — for that unknown someone. "Even if he did it in the middle of the night, I'd think you'd hear something."

"We've been out a lot. There were plenty of times when the house was empty and someone could get in. And with it getting dark as early as it does, why would he bother coming in the middle of the night?"

She digested that. "You think you know, don't you?"

He shook his head. "Somebody comes to mind. It's the sort of thing Carr might do, don't you think?"

"But he's —"

"Dead. I know. But this could have been done at any time. That's the beauty of it. Someone could do it and then just wait for me to have a reason to go down the cellar. No need to be anywhere near here when I fell."

"It might not have been you." A shiver went through her. "It could have been Court. Or me."

Would she have gone down into the cellar, if she'd been alone with Court and the lights went out? Of course she would have. Carr, if it had been he, hadn't seemed to care much who he hurt. But there was another possibility.

The secret Aunt Kate had confided hung heavy on her soul. She'd made the decision to tell him before the accident, but that had intervened. Now, she wasn't so sure. It might have had nothing to do with Annabel's death, and it would hurt Marc so much. And if Draydon found out, he'd think it gave Marc the perfect motive for murder.

"If he wanted me to leave Charleston, it probably didn't really matter to him who got hurt." His face was so tight it looked like a mask, but a muscle twitched under the raw abrasion at his temple.

She couldn't give him something else to worry about, not tonight. Surely bad news could wait a little longer.

She touched his arm, reassured at the feel of warm skin and hard muscle. "I know you don't want to talk to Draydon, but you have to tell him this."

"I know. I will." He closed his hand over hers for a moment. "But not tonight. Court needs time to get over his scare before we're plunged into having police in the house. In the morning is time enough."

"I suppose." But she certainly wouldn't be sleeping tonight.

Marc stood and held out his hand to her. She took it, and he helped her rise. Then he turned away to shut and bolt the cellar door. He spoke without looking at her.

"I think it's time for you to go home and get some sleep. We'll be fine." His tone was coolly dismissive, as if he talked to an employee.

Anger flickered through her, warming her. "Nice try. I promised the doctor I'd stay, and I haven't changed my mind."

"Dinah . . ."

"No!" Aware she'd raised her voice, she glanced up the stairs, but there was no sound from Court. "I'm going to make myself a cup of tea, and then I'm going to curl up on the couch in the family room. Please go to bed. I'll be checking on you through the night, just as the doctor ordered."

She waited for an argument. It didn't come. Marc just stared at her for a long moment. Then he turned and went quietly up the stairs.

She let out a shaky breath. It could have been worse, although what could be worse than having Marc look at her as if she were an irritating stranger?

Please, Lord. I don't know what to do about this. I'm afraid for Marc. I don't know where to turn. Please, hold us in Your hands tonight.

Somehow just the act of prayer calmed her fears. She went steadily across the hall to double-check the lock on the front door. Everything was safe.

As it had been safe the night Annabel died? She couldn't let herself think about that, or she'd never get through this night.

She walked quickly past the side table. The jasmine had been replaced with a spray of greens and holly. It didn't matter. It still reminded her of Annabel.

FOURTEEN

The night had been peaceful, but Dinah certainly didn't look it. She frowned at her reflection in her bedroom mirror the next morning. She patted some concealer on the dark shadows under her eyes and dusted powder over it. That would have to do for the moment.

She glanced at her daybook as she tucked it in her bag. Tomorrow was Christmas Eve. She seemed to have lost a few days from this Advent season in the turmoil of the past few days.

Well, Christmas would come whether she felt ready or not. It didn't depend on how many gifts she had wrapped.

Her cell phone rang, and she hurried to pick it up from the dresser, heart thumping. How long until she didn't react to every unexpected sound?

"Hello?"

"Hey, girlfriend, saddle up. Teresa's ready

to talk to you." Tracey didn't bother to hide her exuberance.

"Seriously?" That was unexpected.

"You bet. How soon can you meet me there?"

"Half an hour. Frankly, I'm surprised the captain was willing to let you use me, after everything that's happened."

Tracey's hesitation gave her away. "Let's say that what the captain doesn't know won't hurt any of us."

"I don't want you to risk your job for me."

Tracey chuckled. "Don't worry. All I'm risking is a chewing out. And if we get anything, it'll be worth it. See you there."

If they got anything. Dinah grabbed her bag and headed for the stairs.

Please, Lord. Let us bring some closure to this situation, for Teresa's sake, at least.

Once she was in the car, fighting the morning traffic that was inevitable in a small city hemmed in by two rivers, she let herself think about Marc. He was meeting with Draydon this morning. She'd offered to be there and had been turned down so curtly that it was almost an insult.

Her feelings didn't matter. All that mattered was that Lieutenant Draydon see that someone was after Marc. That he take it seriously. Draydon might begin from the suspicion that Marc was guilty, but head-quarters scuttlebutt said he was a fair man. That was the best they could hope for, wasn't it?

She pulled to the curb behind Tracey's car, greeted her and went back up the narrow, dirty stairs, her heart beating faster now, her hands clammy. Would this be the day they got something?

Once again the anxious-looking mother ushered them in, and once again Dinah took her seat at the table across from the girl, pad in her lap. Teresa wrapped her arms around her thin body, staring down at the plastic lace place mat in front of her.

"I'm glad you wanted to talk to me again, Teresa." She kept her voice low. "Can we talk about that day again?"

Teresa shot her a dark, unreadable look. "Don't you want to ask me what he looked like?"

This was a little unusual for Teresa. Some witnesses jumped to that right away, but not the difficult ones. Not the ones she was called in on.

"If you want to tell me."

She shook her head. "I've told you and told you. I've told everyone. I didn't see him. Or if I did, I don't remember."

But her voice, her manner, cried out to

Dinah's heart.

Please, Father. Help me to help her.

"Let's just talk about that day, then. Talk about what you did see."

Back to the beginning. Talk about the day her friend died, lead her through all the small, mundane happenings of the day, the things that seemed ordinary at the time but now took on new meaning, viewed from the context of what they knew had happened that evening.

Teresa began to relax — she could see it in the way her fingers unclenched. More detail crept into her narrative. Who had spoken to them at lunch, what they'd said, who'd already seen the movie they'd planned to attend.

Almost without her recognizing it, Dinah's pencil began to move. She held her breath, forcing herself not to stare down at the page. Sometimes it happened this way, as if God were letting her see through the words, see what the witness had seen, live it through her.

Hard. It was hard. Her breath quickened when Teresa's did. Her hands grew clammy, and her stomach lurched when the girls turned into the alley.

A dark figure, a scuffle, a scream — her own scream, or was it Teresa's? Fragments of details coming out almost without Teresa seeming to know it. A smell, the brush of fabric from a jacket, the sound of labored breathing. The knowing. Close your eyes, don't look, you must never know —

Dinah's pencil raced, emotion flooding through her body, into her fingers. Choking her.

Teresa stopped, as if a switch had been turned off. Her hands went to her mouth, her eyes glistening. "I can't." She started to push away from the table, ready to flee.

"Not yet." She didn't take her gaze from the girl. "Tracey, will you get her mother, please?"

Tracey moved. She heard the murmur of voices from the bedroom, their footsteps coming back. She held Teresa in place with sheer force of will.

When they were all there, she spoke. "Teresa." She lifted the drawing pad, heavy now with the weight of grief. "Is this the man?" She held it so the girl could see.

Teresa stared, face horrified. She let out an anguished cry, echoed by her mother. "Yes. Yes." She collapsed onto the table, sobs wrenching her body. Her mother gave a keening cry and held her.

Tracey's focus moved from the drawing to the school photos on the wall. "The brother?"

Her throat was so choked she could barely get the words out. "Yes. She'll tell you now. She'll tell you."

She turned and fled from the room.

Dinah could only thank God that she didn't have to deal with the aftermath of their discovery, as Tracey did. She pulled the car into the garage and hurried through the back gate into the garden. The sky, dark and lowering, seemed to echo her feelings, looking as if it would burst into tears at any moment.

Was I right to expose the truth, Father? She wrapped her jacket around her as she scurried toward the door. *It's going to bring so much grief for them. Maybe it would be better never to know.*

She didn't know. All she knew was that she wanted to collapse into bed and fall into a deep, dreamless sleep. That seemed very unlikely. Sleep, yes, but dreamless? She shivered as she pulled the door open. Dreams came with the territory for her.

She hurried into the dim hallway and nearly ran into Marc. Her breath caught, and she tried to arrange her face into something that wouldn't give away her feelings.

"Marc. I didn't realize you were here."

"Just checking on Court, but don't tell him I said so. He's in the kitchen with Alice and your aunt, helping them bake pies. Or getting in the way, I'm not sure which."

"They're delighted to have him, I know." She edged past him. If she could just reach the stairs without letting him get a good look at her face, she could escape.

"Dinah?" He caught her arm. "What is it? You look as if you've been hit by a truck."

She tried to smile. "That's an interesting comment coming from a man with your bruises."

His hand slid to her wrist, his fingers encircling it. Could he feel the way her pulse hammered? Probably.

"You're shaking." He checked around, seeming to know instinctively that she wouldn't want to run into Aunt Kate just now. "Come with me." He led her into the front parlor, closed the door and nearly shoved her into a chair.

He sat down opposite her, holding her hand wrapped in his. "Talk. What's going on?"

"I should go upstairs. I don't want Aunt Kate to see me. She has enough prejudice against my work already."

"Something happened at work. Tell me. Is

268

it the case you were working on with the teenage girl?"

Clearly she wasn't getting out of the room without telling him something. "She agreed to see us again. This time . . ." She tried to control the shudder that went through her. "I can't explain it. Sometimes I just get so close to the witness that I react as much to the things they don't say as to what they do."

To her surprise, he nodded. "I know. That happens to me sometimes when I'm questioning a witness or a client. You just know, even before you reason it out."

"You understand. That makes it easier. Some of the detectives look at me as if I'm crazy."

"They do the same thing, probably. They just call it a hunch, or a gut instinct." The gentle movement of his fingers on her hand soothed her. "So you identified the guy. That's good."

"Not so good. It was her brother." Her fingers strained against his. "I can't help but wonder if I did the right thing. What that family will go through —"

"Don't, Dinah, don't. It'll be rough, but they'll be able to heal now, don't you see?"

"I suppose. What a sad Christmas they'll have." Her eyes were hot with unshed tears.

She shook her head. "I'm sorry. I need to go upstairs and lie down for a bit."

She stood, and he rose, too, his face drawn with concern.

"Believe it, Dinah. The truth is always better. Always. You were able to help that girl face it. If you —"

He stopped abruptly, but she knew what he wanted to say.

"Why can't I do the same for myself?" She swung away, hands clenching so tightly her nails cut into her palms. "That's what you mean, isn't it?"

"I guess I do."

She couldn't bear the pity in his voice. "I didn't see anything!" She heard an echo of Teresa's words in her own. "I didn't!" She bolted from the room, running up the stairs as if something chased her.

By the time she reached the top she was breathless. She hurried into her room, shut the door and turned the lock. She never locked herself in her room. Never. But she had to be alone.

The impulse to throw herself on the bed and weep had been displaced by anger. She paced across the room. How could he do that to her? He'd seen how upset she was already. How could he try and make her face that again?

She stalked to the window, staring down at the street. Marc came out of the gate and walked across toward his house. His shoulders were stiff with tension.

She turned away, hot tears spilling onto her cheeks. Her anger slipped away, leaving in its place a frightening emptiness.

She sank into her desk chair, fingers touching the objects on the desk at random. She hadn't even asked him how it went with Draydon. She should have.

Burying her face in her hands, she reached out to God. *I'm sorry. I'm so sorry. Taking my fears out on Marc isn't fair. He just wants to know the truth. But I can't. I can't.*

That was what Teresa had said. She hadn't accepted it from the girl. She'd forced her to go deeper than she'd wanted to do, because they had to know the truth.

Justice. Tracey wouldn't use the word, but that was what drove her. The need for justice in a messy world.

Marc needed justice, too. He was in danger. Feelings didn't matter. She hadn't spared Teresa's feelings, had she? Why was she so protective of her own?

That's different, Father.

But it wasn't. It wasn't, was it? She picked up a pencil, fingers moving aimlessly. How did she justify sparing herself from pain?

She'd spent the past ten years praying to God to let her forget. *For now we see in a glass dimly . . .* She'd wanted to go on seeing dimly. Not knowing.

Was there anything to know? She took a deep, shaking breath. *Please, Father. If there's anything to remember, please let me remember. Let me see clearly.*

She probed delicately into her mind, as carefully as a surgeon with a scalpel. Was there anything? That day — the memories came slipping back as she opened the door to them a crack.

Annabel, irritated at Marc for working late. Irritated at everyone and everything, it seemed. Scolding Court for some small infraction until Dinah had scooped him up, carrying him upstairs for a bath and a story, snuggling with him as if that would make up for Annabel's mood.

Standing outside Court's door, listening. Annabel had been in the parlor. She hadn't wanted to see Annabel again, angry that her grown-up cousin had acted so childishly.

Why are you being such a nag? Marc had to work late. He couldn't help it. You shouldn't act that way toward Court. Don't you realize how sensitive he is?

Shocking, to think those things about Annabel, beautiful, loving Annabel, whom she'd idolized.

Her tears had spilled over. She could feel them on her cheeks now, hot and salty. She'd run into her room, thrown herself on the bed, cried out all the frantic, fervent emotions that tumbled inside her.

Later, much later, something had wakened her. She'd opened the door, standing there with her bare feet on the wooden floor, hesitating. Voices. Someone was with Annabel. Had Marc come home? Were they arguing about his working so much?

She'd crept to the stairs, her hand gripping the railing. She'd leaned over. And then . . .

Nothing. Her mind shrank back, wincing, closing over the wound. Don't go in, don't go in, don't go in.

She clenched the pencil so hard it snapped off in her hand.

Please, God. She stopped, not sure what to pray. And then she knew.

Please, Father. If it's Your will, let me remember. I'm open to whatever You have for me.

Slowly, very slowly, the tension drained out of her. She straightened, wiped her eyes then looked down at the paper on the desk in front of her. And saw what she'd drawn.

It was the Citadel crest, drawn over and

over again across the page.

Marc pushed back from the computer, looking out the study window. It was getting dark already, and he was sitting here with only the glow of the laptop screen for company. He'd managed to lose himself in work for over an hour. He'd managed to forget so easily the pain he'd caused Dinah.

Rotten timing, that's what it had been. He'd known for days that he had to talk to her again about what she might remember from that night, but he'd kept putting it off, not wanting to cause a breach between them.

And now, because he'd been frustrated after that futile conversation with Draydon, he'd brought it up to Dinah at the worst possible moment. She'd already been used up by what must have been a terrible experience for her with the girl, and he'd barged in and trampled on her feelings.

He leaned back, rubbing the nape of his neck. Dinah was stuck in the past, able to help other people bring the memories out and face them, but unable to do the same for herself.

I'd like to believe I did it for her sake, Lord, but I know that's not true. I chose that moment because I'm desperate for something that will clear me. If I'm charged, what will happen to Court?

No excuses. He was making excuses, and there weren't any. *I was wrong. Forgive me. And please, show me what to do, because I'm at the end of my rope. I thought I knew what was right. Now I just don't know.*

He heard a key turn in the lock of the front door. Court, coming in ravenous for supper? Or Dinah? She was the only other person with a key.

He had reached the doorway when Dinah met him. She shoved past him into the study, thrusting a sheet of paper at him. Her face was nearly as white as the page.

"Dinah? What's happened?" He looked at her, not the paper in his hand.

"I tried." Her voice shook. "I tried to do what you wanted, and that's what happened."

He glanced down at the sheet. It was an image of the Citadel crest, done over and over in Dinah's delicate pencil drawing, some a simple doodle of a couple of lines, others shaded and rounded.

"I don't understand." Instinct told him not to approach her. She looked as if she'd shatter like crystal at an unwary touch.

Her eyes, dark with shadows, focused on his face. She took a ragged breath and

275

seemed to search for calm.

"I tried to remember. I opened myself to whatever memories I might have hidden away about that night."

Excitement surged through him, but he forced his voice to remain calm. "Did you remember anything?"

She was looking into the past, her eyes wide, the pupils dilated. "Playing outside with Court on the swings after supper. It was so hot, but he had to be outside. I pushed him. He kept saying, 'Higher, higher.'"

"What happened when you came inside?" Gently. Don't startle her out of the memory.

"He was all sweaty, his hair wet and curling on his neck." She smiled slightly. "I hugged him. We were laughing." The smile slipped away. "Annabel was upset. Angry with you, for not coming home. Angry with me, for letting Court run around outside in the heat. Angry with Court, for putting his dirty hands on her clean skirt."

"It didn't mean anything, sugar. It was really me she was annoyed with, not you and Court." She was hurting. He didn't want her to hurt. But he needed her to remember.

"I know." She shook her head a little, seeming to come back to the present. "But

I got mad at her. It seems so wrong, that I got mad at her and a few hours later she was dead."

"We all felt that way." He longed to put his arms around her in comfort, but he didn't dare. "Did you yell at her?"

She looked shocked. "No, of course not."

Of course not. Shy little Dinah would never have yelled at the grown-up cousin she adored.

"What did you do?"

"I took Court up and gave him a bath. We played, read stories. Afterward . . ." She hesitated for a long moment. "Usually, if you weren't there, I'd go down and watch television with Annabel. But I was still angry with her. So I just went in my bedroom, found a book to read and went to bed."

That explained why Annabel had been alone downstairs. But why had she been in the front parlor? That had never been explained. Then, as now, they used the family room almost exclusively unless they were entertaining.

"You woke up," he said quietly. "At some point, you woke. Do you know what woke you?"

She shook her head, black hair moving against the white cashmere sweater she wore. She'd come out without a coat.

"I was just awake. I thought I heard someone downstairs, so I went to the door. Opened it. I went to the top of the stairs." She stopped. "That's all. That's all I could remember." She closed her eyes for an instant. "But there's something else. Something Aunt Kate told me yesterday."

His heart thudded. He'd been convinced Kate was hiding something from him. He'd been right. "What? What did she say?"

Her lips pressed together, as if she didn't want to let the words out. She swallowed, the muscles in her throat working. "She overheard Annabel on the phone. Talking to a man. She said . . ." She stopped, her mouth twisting.

Shock and pain clawed at his chest. "It can't be."

"She blames herself for not confronting her." Dinah's voice was thick with tears. "She's sure it's true that Annabel was involved with a man that summer."

Another man. How could he have not known, not guessed that something that serious was wrong?

"What about you?" The words came harshly. "Did you know?"

"Of course not. I never imagined anything of the kind."

There was something in her voice that caught at him. He grasped her hands, swinging her around to face him. "Tell me the truth, Dinah."

"I am! I just —" She wrenched her hands free, wiping at her tears like a child. "Ever since you came back, I've felt as if I had to protect her memory. Maybe, somewhere deep, I suspected. I don't know!"

He struggled to stop reacting and start thinking. A man. "Who? Who was around that summer?" He knew the answer to that. The usual group of friends — people he knew well, people he'd never dream would betray him. "This is crazy," he muttered. "She must have been wrong. Aunt Kate. She must have misunderstood."

"I'd like to believe that."

"But you don't." He shot a look at her, irrationally angry with her, as if she were to blame.

She shook her head tiredly. "I don't know, Marc." She nodded toward the crest. "But that has to mean something."

He finally got it. "You think this points to me, don't you? With Annabel's affair providing the motive."

"That's not what I said."

His stomach churned, his finger curling into fists, crumpling the paper. "You didn't have to." He shook the paper at her. "Your drawing says it for you. You identify me with the crest."

She seemed to be looking at him from a great distance. "You used to wear a Citadel tiepin whenever you wore a tie. It was gold. Annabel gave it to you."

"And you'll convict me on that." He wanted to shake her.

Anger flamed suddenly in her eyes. "You're the one who wanted me to remember. I tried, and that's what happened. Don't blame me because I couldn't come up with the answer you wanted."

He wasn't sure when he'd been this angry. Dinah, the one person he was sure believed in him, thought he was guilty.

Carefully he put the paper down on the desk. "You'd better keep this safe. Draydon might want to see it."

"Marc —"

He shook his head, grabbing his jacket from the back of the chair. "I'm going out. Tell Court I'll pick him up later."

Later. As in after he regained control of himself. Without looking at her, he stalked out of the room and out of the house.

FIFTEEN

When the door slammed behind Marc, the house seemed to shudder in response. Dinah sank down in the desk chair and leaned back, head throbbing. Raw emotion still hovered in the tightness of her throat.

But she couldn't cry anymore. She was all cried out. She closed her eyes, tried not to think. She was tired, so tired. Too tired to get up, cross the road to Aunt Kate's, deal with the questions Aunt Kate and Court would have.

So she sat, unwilling to move, unwilling even to think. She'd just rest for a while. Try not to think. Just rest, until she felt able to cope again.

She wasn't sure how long she sat there before the images started to form in her mind. Against the blackness of her closed lids, she saw her bare toes curling into the stair carpeting. Saw her hand reach for the railing. Felt herself lean against the railing, looking down at the hallway.

The white tiles glowed softly in the dim light of the small lamp Annabel kept burning. Voices murmured. The door to the front parlor must be ajar. She couldn't see it from where she stood, but light streamed out in a pale yellow band, crossing the tiles, touching the table, the jasmine, the mirror.

She shot bolt upright, a shudder working its way through her body. She was remembering. After all these years of insisting she'd seen nothing, knew nothing, she was remembering.

She was alone in the house for the first time in years, if ever. Was that why? She gripped the leather arms of the desk chair, holding on as if afraid she'd fall.

Alone in the house. Once this had been a second home, but after Annabel died she'd avoided it as she'd have avoided walking through a cemetery at midnight.

Then Marc and Court came back. That sense had faded, a little painfully, perhaps, but it had gone. She wasn't afraid here any longer.

Because of Marc. That was it. Because at the deepest level of her soul, she wasn't afraid of him. She knew he hadn't been with Annabel in the parlor that night. He hadn't struck out at her.

Whatever that image of the Citadel ring meant, it didn't mean that. Marc had jumped to the conclusion she was accusing him, but —

Wait. Why had she thought of it as a ring? She'd identified it to Marc as the crest, which could have been on any piece of jewelry or clothing.

The paper lay on the desk, where Marc had thrown it. She snatched it up and smoothed it, peering at the drawing in the glow of the computer screen.

She touched the most developed of the drawings, probably the one she'd done last. There — was that the suggestion of a curve, as if the crest were set in a curving band?

It wasn't evidence. Even if she generated a complete memory, which she had no idea if she could do, that wasn't evidence. But to her, it was better than evidence. It was proof. Marc hadn't worn any ring except his wedding ring. So whoever the drawing pointed to, it wasn't Marc.

She pushed herself out of the chair, and moved silently over the soft carpet. She'd go home, pull herself together and find some way of making Marc understand.

Judging by the way he'd rocketed out of the house, that wouldn't be easy. For the first time she realized she was standing in near-dark, with only the glow of the computer screen for light.

She reached toward the lamp, then drew her hand back. Go home. Marc would have to go there to pick up Court. She'd talk to him then.

She went quietly to the door, her feet making no sound on the soft carpet. She opened it and stopped, heart in her throat.

There was a light on in the front parlor. The door was ajar, sending a band of yellow light across the tiles.

A shiver went through her. No voices, not this time. But noise. Someone was in the room, moving around.

Marc? Could he have come quietly back to the house without her hearing him? Well, obviously someone had.

Somehow she didn't want to click across the tile floor in her heels. She slid out of her shoes and picked them up. Then stood, torn with indecision.

If it was Marc in the room, she'd feel like a fool for trying to sneak out of the house without speaking to him. It couldn't be Court. He'd never enter the house or any other place that quietly.

No one else had a key. Whoever had rigged the cellar steps to fall hadn't needed a key.

She'd been a coward for most of her life.

If she didn't at least try to see who was in the parlor, she'd be a coward for the rest of it.

Please, Lord.

She'd slip across the hall, staying in the shadow. Whoever it was, he obviously thought he was alone. Either it was Marc, in which case she had no need to fear. Or it was someone else, and she'd never forgive herself if she didn't try to find out who that someone else was.

Marc sat in his car, staring across the street at The Citadel. True to its name, in the dusk it looked like a medieval citadel, its pale walls glimmering. It had taught generations of cadets the meaning of discipline and honor. It had given him an excellent education and friendships he'd thought would last a lifetime. Now it had also given him a frightening puzzle.

He'd driven around the city in a haze of anger until he'd found himself here, face-to-face with his past. The anger faded, forcing him to recognize how futile and foolish it had been.

Dinah was right. She'd done what he asked, at who knows what cost to her psyche. She'd told him the truth about Annabel, even though it ripped her apart with pain. And he'd repaid her with anger.

Somehow the idea that Dinah believed in him had become a part of his assumptions about himself. About her. The fear that she didn't trust him had rocked him more than he'd have believed possible.

Because he considered her his only friend here? No.

Truth time. It wasn't friendship he felt for Dinah. Without realizing it, his feelings for her had deepened over the past weeks into love.

Hopeless love, probably. He'd known from the first surge of attraction that there could be no future for them. The only thing he could do that might help Dinah to heal was to get to the bottom of this.

All right. Dinah had brought back some images of that night, and the crest was part of that. The only thing he had to work on, in fact. But he began with the knowledge that he hadn't killed Annabel. So the implication of the crest was that the person who'd been in the house that night hadn't been an ex-con like Hassert or a casual worker like Carr.

It had been a friend. Who? The man Aunt Kate heard her talking to?

His eyes closed. They'd entertained that summer, but not much. Annabel had said she was too tired much of the time. But when they did have people over, the crowd had inevitably included two people who had reason to wear a ring or a tiepin with that insignia. James. And Phillips.

His friends. The three musketeers.

But James could barely manage to be civil to him now. Because he thought Marc had killed Annabel? Or because of his own fear and guilt because he'd done it?

His stomach churned, his hands tightening on the wheel. Dinah had said that James cared for Annabel. He'd never realized that. How was it that the naive teenager had seen what he hadn't? Could Annabel have come to return those feelings? Had a lovers' quarrel turned deadly?

His instinct was to rush to James's office and confront him, but what good would that do? He had no evidence, nothing that would remotely convince Draydon, for instance. Just Dinah's drawing and a barely realized memory. And Draydon would be far more likely to consider that he now had motive, means, and opportunity against Marc.

Phillips wore a Citadel ring. The thought drifted through his mind and then clung like a burr. Not Phillips. It couldn't have been. Phillips was one person who could have had no possible reason to harm Annabel. He hadn't been attracted to her — just the opposite, in fact. He'd been polite to her, but made it clear in his subtle way that he thought her an idle debutante with nothing more serious in her head than the next cotillion.

And Annabel had dismissed Phillips as stuffy, stuck in the past, unable to talk about anything but his beloved history.

He shook his head, trying to clear it. He was groping in a fog, trying to come up with scenarios that would explain the inexplicable. There was only one reasonable next step. He had to go back to Dinah, apologize, and convince her to probe more deeply.

Something had put the image of the crest into her mind, projected it through her clever fingers. The memory had to be there, if only she could access it.

He pulled out his cell phone. Apologize. He'd treated Dinah badly, raging out at her that way. He had to make up for that. He was forming the phrases in his mind when he realized the phone had gone straight to Dinah's voice mail.

He clicked off. This was not a message that could be delivered via voice mail. He had to talk to her in person.

She'd be at Kate's, of course. It was dinnertime. He'd go there, he'd apologize, and

Dinah would forgive him. He couldn't let himself envision any other possibility.

The door to the parlor stood ajar. She'd taken a long time to cross the hallway, step by cautious step, holding her shoes in one hand. She stopped a few inches from the door, barely breathing.

It wasn't too late. She could back away as quietly as she'd come. Go out the back door, run for help. Call the police, call Marc —

If she hadn't rushed out of the house that way, with nothing in her hand but that drawing, she'd have her cell phone. But she'd been acting on instinct, knowing she had to get to Marc.

That in itself showed that she'd known he couldn't have killed Annabel. She hadn't taken the time to see that, and Marc had been so shocked that he'd jumped to the worst possible conclusion. He'd recognize that, as soon as he calmed down enough to think. He'd put that analytical mind of his to work figuring out what the crest meant.

But she would know. Because she wasn't going to back away. She was going to find out who was in that room.

She leaned close to the crack of the door. She could see a sliver of the room — the fireplace, with its ornate mantel and gilt-framed mirror. The tall secretary desk that had once stood in Annabel's bedroom, brought down from the attic to make the room look furnished.

The front flap of the desk lay open. Someone stood in front of it. She could see part of a dark-jacketed shoulder, an arm.

Not Marc, then. He'd gone rushing out without a coat, and his sweater had been a cream fisherman's knit. But she'd known that all along, at some level.

She had to see who it was. Palm resting gently on the panel, she pushed the door wide enough to see the curve of neck, the fair, slightly graying hair. He was bent over the desk, looking at something she couldn't see.

She must have made some sound, perhaps the faintest gasp. He swung toward her.

"Dinah!" Phillips tried to smile, but it was an awkward twitch of the lips. "Goodness, you startled me. I thought there was no one home."

Too late now to run away. But Phillips — Annabel's killer couldn't be Phillips, could it?

"I was in the study." She got the words out through stiff lips and forced herself to step inside the room. To do anything else would look unnatural. If she bolted toward the door, he could be on her in an instant.

Act. Pretend. Make him believe you don't suspect a thing.

He gestured toward the desk. "I wanted to find a pen and paper, so I could leave a note for Marc. Do you know when he'll be back?"

Her mind raced. Was it better for him to believe Marc would show up at any moment? Or might that precipitate the very action she wanted to avoid?

"I don't know." She attempted a smile. "Court is over at Aunt Kate's, and dinner is almost ready. I'm sure Marc will show up soon."

Better. She sounded almost normal, didn't she? She turned, oh so casually, toward the door.

"I'd best get back to the house before Aunt Kate sends Court over to fetch me. I think you'll find a pen and paper on Marc's desk."

Her gaze hit the gilt-framed mirror over the mantel. The mirror reflected her face, chalk-white. Phillips standing by the desk, straightening his glasses in a characteristic gesture, the glint of the ring on his hand.

She froze, unable to speak, to move. She knew. Beyond all doubt, she knew.

"Oh, Dinah." He sounded grieved. "I can't let you go anywhere now."

Please, Lord, let me get out of here.

"Phillips, I don't know . . ." She swung her head to look at him, and the words died in her throat.

Still smiling that vague, scholarly smile, Phillips pulled a gun out of his pocket and pointed it at her.

Sixteen

"She's not here?" Marc stared blankly at Court, who'd opened the door. Behind him, in the hallway, Kate peered nervously over his shoulder.

"I haven't seen her all afternoon," Court said. "Dad? Is something wrong?"

"She didn't come back here?" Where was Dinah? She should be here. "She didn't come back about an hour ago?"

Court shook his head. "I told you. We haven't seen her since she went out ages ago."

Kate's lips began to tremble. She put her hand on Court's arm, and he turned instantly to support her. Even in the grasp of blinding fear for Dinah, Marc was glad to see the bond between them.

"What's happened?" Kate's voice wavered, sounding as old as her years. "Has something happened to Dinah?"

No point in lying now, even to spare her

feelings. The fear had turned into a drum-beat, thundering in his head.

Dinah hadn't come back. She hadn't come back from the house. Something had happened.

He grasped Court's arm. "Call the police. Send them to the house. Hurry!"

He spun, racing across the veranda, taking the path in a few quick strides. *Please, God, please, God, please, God.* The prayer echoed in rhythm with his feet.

He shoved the gate open and raced into the street, blood pounding in his head. A nightmare. It was a nightmare. He'd dreamed a thousand times of reaching the house in time to save Annabel. He never had.

Father, let me be in time to save Dinah. I have to. Please. Please.

Through the gate, up the walk, hurry, hurry. He pounded across the veranda, reached for the door. No time to slip in undetected — he didn't dare take the time for that. He might already be too late.

His momentum took him through the door, into the hall, toward the study where he'd left her —

He skidded to a stop.

Lights in the parlor. Voices, apparently undeterred by his noisy entrance.

Voices. Dinah's voice. Relief left him weak for an instant. *Thank You, God. Thank You.* She was alive. He wouldn't rush in and find her lying cold and still, as he'd found Annabel.

Two strides took him to the door, standing half-open. He thrust it the rest of the way, took a step into the room and stopped. Stared.

Dinah stood a few feet away from him, stiff with tension. She didn't turn to look at him, because her eyes were focused on the person who stood across the room.

Phillips smiled at him, the same grave, gentle smile that had been part of his life for years and years. The only thing out of place was the gun in his hand, pointing directly at Dinah.

"Marc. I didn't want you to come. I wanted to be finished with this, but it's all gone wrong." The smile wavered. "I never meant for this to happen."

Marc took a step closer to Dinah. He had to get her behind him, give her a few precious seconds to get out the door if Phillips used the gun.

"What didn't you want to happen, Phil?" He kept his voice calm, unthreatening. "Why don't you let me take that gun, and then we can sit down and talk about this?"

Phillips glanced down at the gun as if he'd forgotten he held it. He looked back up again at Marc's unwary step toward him.

"No, Marc. I can't. I can't put it down. There isn't any other way out. I've gone too far." He shook his head again, and tears shone in his eyes behind the glasses.

"He killed Annabel." Dinah's voice was hardly more than a whisper. "I heard them arguing. I stood on the steps, but I wasn't sure who it was."

For the moment he almost forgot Phil and the gun. All he could see was Dinah's pale face and huge eyes.

"It's all right, sugar." He closed the space between them, heedless of the gun, and clasped her cold hands in his. "You don't have to remember."

"I remember. I know what I saw." Her eyes flickered toward the mirror over the mantel. "I saw the reflection of his hand, reflected again in the hall mirror. I saw the ring he wore."

"You didn't remember. No one knew. You shouldn't have remembered."

Phil's voice had gone shrill. He was losing control. How much longer before he fired the gun?

"What about Jasper Carr?" He had to divert Phil's attention from Dinah. "The way he was acting, he must have seen something." And now Carr was dead. This was unreal. Phil, Phil of all people, couldn't be a murderer.

The gun wavered slightly, as if Phil's hand was growing tired. "He saw me near the house. He didn't know anything, not really. I paid him to go away."

"Carr came back, though, didn't he? And you had to deal with him."

"Only because you came to Charleston."

His voice shook, and so did the gun. Fear jerked tighter. They could be just as dead if Phil fired accidentally.

"You're getting tired, Phil. Let's put the gun down and talk."

He shook his head, tears beginning to flow down his cheeks. "Why did you come back? I was so happy to see you, to be with my best friend again, but then it all started to unravel."

"It's too late. We both know that. The truth has to come out." He was taking a risk, but what choice did he have? He stepped in front of Dinah, pushing her back a step, putting his body between her and the gun.

"No! No, I can't face it. What will Margo say? What will everyone say? How can I live with the shame?"

"You're already living with the shame. You know that. You're tired of it." He took a step toward Phillips, holding out his hand. "Give me the gun now."

"I can't!" He sounded like that boy they'd dragged through the obstacle course.

He reached for the gun. "Come on, now, Phil. The only way out would be to shoot both of us, and you know you can't do that."

He held his breath, his mind a wordless prayer. If Phil turned the gun toward Dinah, he was close enough to jump him. Dinah would take care of Court, if it came to that.

The gun steadied, the barrel pointed directly at him. He didn't move, didn't breathe, just stared into the face of his old friend.

Slowly, very slowly, the gun lowered.

"No." Phillips managed a smile. "You're right. You were always right, Marc. I can't." He slid to the floor, curling his arms around his knees.

When the police burst through the door a few minutes later, he didn't even look up.

Dinah waited in Aunt Kate's parlor, fingers clasped around a cup of tea. Court was upstairs in bed, asleep, she hoped. Aunt Kate had tried to persuade her to take a sedative and go to bed, but she'd refused and kept on refusing, as gently as possible.

She didn't want to sleep, or be cosseted, or treated like a child. Marc would come as soon as he'd finished with the police and with Margo. Margo might not want his help, but she'd have it, because she was Phillips's wife.

She shoved her hair back wearily. Odd, how very odd it all was. She'd wanted to hate the person who robbed them of Annabel, but all she could feel for Phillips was pity. He was like a sick child.

The door clicked, and Marc came in. He hesitated on the threshold for a moment. He looked as if he'd been through agony. He had.

He came to sit next to her. His very presence seemed to bring warmth to the room.

"I thought you might have gone to bed."

"No. I needed to know."

Marc took her hand in his, holding it lightly, seeming hardly aware that he'd done so. "He's talking. As an attorney, I advised him not to say anything, but he wouldn't stop talking. I think he was just so tired of trying to hide it all these years."

"It takes a lot of energy to hide the truth." She should know that, even though her efforts had been beyond her conscious control. "He and Annabel — did they really have an affair?"

Let it all come out. Let the truth be said between them, even if the rest of the world never knew.

Marc nodded. "Funny." He gave the breath of a laugh. "I thought it was James. Once I started to think about the crest, I was convinced it was James."

He was still hurting, so much. She wanted to soothe the pain away, but this was beyond comfort. They'd just have to endure it.

"James cared about her, I think." Carefully. Don't make matters any worse. "He thought you'd killed her. That's why he was so hateful to you."

"I didn't even think Phil and Annabel liked each other. He and Margo had been having problems, and Annabel — well, I think mostly Annabel was bored and angry." He gave her a sideways glance. "Does my saying that upset you?"

"No."

At some point, she'd realized how it must have been. Maybe she'd always known, but she hadn't been able to admit it.

"I loved her. I love her still." She struggled to understand and put the feelings into words. "But I don't have to think her perfect any longer. She was just a fallible human being, like the rest of us."

His fingers tightened on hers. "I'm glad you can see that. It will make it easier, eventually."

"There's a lot to go through before that happens. The papers will have a field day." More to endure. Somehow Aunt Kate had to be protected from the worst of it.

"Poor Phil. I think he was telling the truth when he said he never meant any of it to happen. He wanted to end it, but Annabel threatened to tell me. She was in that kind of mood — ready to smash something, even if it hurt her, too."

"Yes." She could see it so clearly now, in everything Annabel had said and done that long, hot summer. "I imagine he panicked. He struck out at her and realized too late what he'd done."

Marc's fingers clenched, then relaxed. "He thought he was in the clear when you didn't speak and Carr went away, but he worried about the letters."

"Letters?"

He nodded. "Apparently he wrote love letters to Annabel. How like Phillips that was, wasn't it? Indulging in some romantic dream, as if he and Annabel were Lancelot and Guinevere."

They hadn't been. They'd just been a willful, spoiled young woman and a weak man.

She felt an eternity older than Annabel had been.

"So that's what he was looking for in the secretary. His letters."

"Apparently he never thought he could risk searching for them when the house was rented. But when I came back and Carr reappeared, he got desperate."

"He killed Carr." Her voice choked a little. "I'm the one who told him Carr was back in town. He was there when I asked James if he remembered Carr. If I hadn't mentioned it, Carr might still be alive."

Marc shook his head, frowning. "Don't think that. Carr had blackmailed him once and was apparently trying it again. It wasn't your fault."

"I still can't believe he killed Carr in cold blood." An impulsive crime of passion, maybe, but not this ugly premeditation.

"He provided the drugs and alcohol. Carr did the rest himself." His voice was dry. "He never intended that I should be blamed. That was pure accident, apparently."

A tiny spurt of fresh anger went through her. "He should have realized they'd suspect you." Her sympathy for Phillips was evaporating. He hadn't thought of anyone but himself from first to last, and too many people had paid for that.

Marc's fingers tightened on hers, as if he guessed her thoughts. "Anyway, he was still afraid I'd stumble across the letters in getting the house ready for sale. That was what he was doing. He thought the house was empty, and he was looking for his letters."

"Were there any letters?"

"No." His shoulders moved slightly. "She probably destroyed them ten years ago."

"The guilty flee where no man pursues," she murmured.

"Exactly." Fresh pain crossed his face. "I'd like to keep their affair from Court, but I don't suppose I'll be able to."

"Court is a very strong young man. He'll be fine."

"Yes." He glanced at the mantel clock and then got to his feet. "It's late. I'd better go home and let you get to bed."

"You're not going back there to sleep. We have a room ready for you here."

Don't go, Marc. Stay with me.

He shook his head. "I'll be fine. I'll come back for breakfast, if Aunt Kate wants me."

"Of course." She fixed a smile on her face. That was it, then. They were to go back to being cousins, apparently.

Ironic. She finally felt free of the past and ready to move on, but all Marc wanted to do was walk away.

She went with him to the door. They might never be alone together again. "Good night, Marc."

The mantel clock chimed the hour. Marc looked into her face.

"It's midnight. It's officially Christmas Eve, Dinah. Merry Christmas." He bent and kissed her quickly, lightly, and then walked away, taking her heart with him.

"It's beautiful, Court." Dinah folded the tissue paper over the lacy sweater and leaned across to kiss Court's cheek. He grinned and reddened but didn't dodge away.

"I couldn't ask for a lovelier Christmas morning than this." Aunt Kate beamed at all of them impartially, as if Marc and Court had been part of their Christmases forever. They were celebrating in Marc's family room, since Court insisted on unwrapping presents beneath the tree.

And, as Aunt Kate said, they may as well get over whatever uncomfortable feelings they had about the house. Celebrating Christmas there would go a long way toward doing that.

They'd gone to the early worship service together. She'd stood next to Marc, singing the joyful Christmas songs, and forced herself to keep smiling, in spite of the pain.

When the legalities were finished, Marc and Court would go back to Boston. They'd come back for visits, of course, but it wouldn't be the same. They wouldn't really be part of one another's lives.

And to Marc she'd go on being what she'd always been — Annabel's little cousin.

"This one's from both Dad and me." Court thrust a long envelope, adorned with a slightly lopsided red bow, into her lap. "Open it next, okay?"

She nodded, slipping her finger under the flap. She looked up at them questioning. "A plane ticket?"

"Not just a ticket." Court beamed. "It's a ticket to Boston that you can use anytime. You have to come and visit us."

She managed not to let the smile slip. "That is so nice. I've always wanted to see Boston in the springtime. You can show me all the sights." She stood quickly. "Now I'm going to bring in some coffee and hot chocolate. Opening gifts is thirsty work."

Nobody would know how hard it was to keep smiling as she hurried out of the room. She'd reached the kitchen before she heard him behind her.

"I can manage this." She clinked cups onto a tray. "You don't have to help me."

"I didn't come to help." Marc took her hands in his, turning her to face him. "I came to talk."

She couldn't look at him, for fear he'd see the hopeless love in her eyes. "I should take this tray in. They'll want to finish opening gifts."

"They'll wait. We've spent the past thirty-six hours surrounded by either family or police. I thought I'd never get you alone again, and I'm not giving that up too easily."

Her heart was thudding so loudly she could barely speak over it. She focused on the top button of his shirt. "We were alone the other night."

"We were both still shaking the other night. I couldn't tell you what I need to say until you'd had a chance to recover a little. Dinah, will you please look at me?"

She lifted her gaze to his, and the warmth in his eyes set an answering warmth flooding through her. "I don't need recovery time. I've spent my life recovering. Now I want to spend it living."

Aunt Kate would be shocked if she heard her. A lady should always wait to be asked.

"That's what I want, too." He lifted her hands to his lips and kissed them. "You must know that I love you. And not as a

Dear Reader,

I'm so glad you decided to pick up this story, the third of my Lowcountry romantic suspense novels. It's been such a pleasure to write these books that I hate to see them come to an end. I loved writing about Dinah and Marcus, and I've begun to feel as if the next time I'm in Charleston, I'll probably see them!

It's always a joy to go back to the Lowcountry of the Georgia and South Carolina coast, the setting for my earlier Caldwell Clan series. It's a beautiful area, filled with mystery and romance as well as with friendly people who love to make you feel at home.

This story is set in Charleston, South Carolina, and I hope you'll enjoy this armchair visit. I fell in love with Charleston when one of my daughters was in graduate school there, and now that she and her family live there, we have a chance to visit more often.

I hope you'll write and let me know how you liked this story. Address your letter to me at Steeple Hill Books, 233 Broadway, Suite 1001, New York, NY 10279, and I'll be happy to send you a signed bookplate or bookmark. You can visit me on the Web at www.martaperry.com or e-mail me at marta@martaperry.com.

Blessings,
Marta Perry

QUESTIONS FOR DISCUSSION

1. Grief over the loss of a loved one can take many forms. Aunt Kate doesn't talk about Annabel, while Dinah has nightmares. How else might they have dealt with their grief?

2. Court's attempts to protect her both amuse and touch Dinah. Have you seen a young teen act in an unusually mature way in an emergency? What do you think gives a young person that ability?

3. Dinah prays that God will keep her from remembering Annabel's death. Her prayer isn't answered in the way she wants, but God gives her the strength to cope with the results. Has God denied a prayer of yours? Have you later seen God's wisdom in that?

4. In the scriptural theme, Paul tells us that

now we see in a glass dimly, but one day we'll see face-to-face. What do you think he means? Have you ever felt you were seeing dimly when you tried to understand God's working in your life?

5. How is the scriptural theme shown in the story? Through which characters and situations?

6. When Marc comes home to Charleston, he realizes how much he's missed it, even while seeing things differently. Have you experienced going back to a place you loved after a long absence? How did it make you feel?

7. Some of Charleston's unique Christmas traditions are mentioned in the story. If a stranger came to your town, what interesting Christmas traditions would she find?

8. Christmas food means cheese bennes and pecan tassies in Charleston. What are some of your traditional Christmas recipes? Do they have special meaning to you because of the person who gave them to you or because you remember them from childhood?

9. Marc blames himself for the problems he and Annabel had. Is this common in your experience? How does one get past this?

10. In the end, Marc and Dinah both have to accept the betrayal of a friend and plan for a life together that will be complex because of their responsibilities. How do you think they can work that out?

ABOUT THE AUTHOR

Marta Perry has written everything from Sunday school curriculum to travel articles to magazine stories in twenty years of writing, but she feels she's found her home in the stories she writes for Love Inspired.

Marta lives in rural Pennsylvania, but she and her husband spend part of each year at their second home in South Carolina. When she's not writing, she's probably visiting her children and her beautiful grandchildren, traveling or relaxing with a good book.

Marta loves hearing from readers and she'll write back with a signed bookplate or bookmark. Email her at marta@marta perry.com, or visit her on the Web at www. martaperry.com.

The employees of Thorndike Press hope you have enjoyed this Large Print book. All our Thorndike and Wheeler Large Print titles are designed for easy reading, and all our books are made to last. Other Thorndike Press Large Print books are available at your library, through selected bookstores, or directly from us.

For information about titles, please call:
  (800) 223-1244

or visit our Web site at:
  www.gale.com/thorndike
  www.gale.com/wheeler

To share your comments, please write:
  Publisher
  Thorndike Press
  295 Kennedy Memorial Drive
  Waterville, ME 04901